TRIBAL SCARS

TRIBAL SCARS
and other stories

Sembène Ousmane

Translated from the French by Len Ortzen
Introduction by Charles R. Larson

A Black Orpheus Press / Inscape Book

INSCAPE
Washington, D.C.

Published by arrangement with Présence Africaine and
Heinemann Educational Books Ltd.

Library of Congress Cataloging in Publication Data

Ousmane, Sembene.
    Tribal scars, and other stories.

    Translation of Voltaique, La Noire de . . . nouvelles.
    I. Title.
PZ3.09445Tr [PQ3989.08]   843   73–21642
ISBN 0–87953–015–4

Contents

Introduction

What has always impressed me most about Sembène Ousmane is his amazing versatility. He is a man of multiple talents and interests—a man who has worked hard much of his life (often at menial tasks) in order to be able to pursue his creative interests. Born in Senegal in 1923 (a Wolof, from the north of Dakar), Ousmane's interests have largely been shaped by the many different jobs he held in his early life: mason, plumber, truck driver, soldier, stevedore, labor leader, and, much later in life, writer and film maker. Indeed, it is as a film maker that he has been best known in America, having produced several prize-winning films.

Largely self-educated, Ousmane's writings and films have often depicted Senegalese people less successful than he: the poor and the downtrodden, the illiterate, the exploited masses. Ousmane would be the first to admit that this exploitation has not been strictly an African versus colonial conflict, though many of his early writings are set during the colonial era. The social injustices have continued, Ousmane believes, years after Senegal's independence from France. There are not enough jobs for the young; some of the new African leaders have become carbon copies of the French (who still number 30,000 in Dakar alone.) Many of Ousmane's criticisms, of course, have been embarrassing to the Senegalese government, and they may account for his relative lack of popularity in certain parts of West Africa. As recently as 1971 when he was visiting the United States, Ousmane was interviewed by a writer for *The New Yorker* and had this to say (in the September 21st issue) about life in Dakar, the Senegalese capital:

Dakar *seems* prosperous . . . but beneath the appearances people are actually poorer than they were before independence. During the colonial period, for example, all medical services were free and quick. Now people have to wait forever, and there are few medicines available. Our desires for modernization outrage reality, and we end up with a capitalistic system that produces very little. There is a housing program that has made money for a small group of people, and there are factories—run by the French—that employ a handful of Africans. But the banks, the industries, the wholesale markets are still controlled by the French, who are forgiven their taxes because they supply jobs, and are permitted to take their profits out of the country. I have noticed that when rich nations—France, Britain, the United States, Japan, Germany—help underdeveloped countries, they always gain more for themselves than they give away.

The stories in this collection—published originally in French by Présence Africaine—clearly illustrate Ousmane's versatility and ability to shape many of the raw experiences of his life into artistic realities. I can think of no other collection of short stories by an African writer that illustrates such variety. Reading them for the first time in English, I became intensely aware of Ousmane's almost unique position in African literature: he has given us (particularly those of us who are not African) the chance to embrace a wide range of African experiences, to understand the whole of African life from pre-colonial times down through the frustrations of the post-independent era.

We have, for example, in this volume, a story called "The Community"—an animal tale, illustrating Ousmane's knowledge of traditional African folklore, the oral literature. Ousmane is, after all, a latter-day figuration of the traditional African storyteller, the griot.

In one of the most remarkable stories in the collection, "Tribal Scars," Ousmane asks the question, "Why do we have tribal scars?" The story itself takes us back several hundred years into the African past—when white slavers were just beginning to decimate the West African coastal areas. While it beautifully illustrates the African sense of sacredness for life, "Tribal Scars" is also a bloody tale of white terror and of one proud African's reaction to the European invasion. The hero, Amoo, kills his wife, rather than permit her to be captured by the slavers. Later he disfigures his daughter, for a similar reason, so she will be of no value to the slavers, thus suggesting that the ritual act of scarring began as an act of defiance and became a symbol of African strength and pride.

Whether Ousmane's speculations about the origin of tribal scars are historically accurate, I cannot say. One thing is clear, however. "Tribal Scars" is a powerful commentary on the inhumanities of slavery, a statement emblematic of the entire African/Western confrontation. The tribal scarifications that many Africans regard as markings of great beauty have become a symbol of the black man's ingenuity for survival, for endurance.

In "Tribal Scars" Ousmane attacks slavery, a subject which many think is now passé, but in doing so, he indirectly assaults the Western world as a whole. However, we have only to examine a number of his other stories in this collection to see that, unrelenting social critic that he is, Ousmane is also a harsh critic of political institutions in Senegal *after* independence. We notice this most clearly in his story, "Love in Sandy Lane," which concludes with a particularly bitter comment about life in Dakar now that the colonial government has left.

In one of the shortest stories in this volume, and one of the best ("In the Face of History") we see Ousmane putting up with no nonsense from those Africans who have embraced Western life and values without questioning their merits. In the original French edition, "In the Face of History" was given a more prominent position; it appeared as the first story in the collection. Every time I re-read it, I am amazed at its subtlety—achieved so remarkably in less than four pages. As the story opens, three African males (presumably Muslims) are standing out in front of a local cinema, looking at the marquee. One of them says to the others, "If you see that film, you'll never in your life be able to trust a woman again . . . ." The movie, we shortly learn, is *Samson and Delilah,* certainly a cultural shock for Africans who often have a more rigidly defined code for male/female relationships than Americans have.

As the three African men comment on the film, a taxi draws up in front of the theatre, ejecting an African couple dressed in European clothes. Most of the rest of the story is concerned with an argument the couple have in front of the theatre. The husband doesn't want to see the film because he says they have already seen it before. The wife doesn't think that matters. After all, it is Saturday night, and, as she tells him, " 'I don't want to waste my time with your pals who do nothing but talk about their game of cards . . . .' " When their argument ends, husband and wife go their separate ways. That leaves the three African males still standing in front of the cinema. Then they leave, since there is no reason to pay to see the film. They have just seen *Samson and Delilah* acted out in front of them for free.

This is not to suggest that Ousmane thinks women have no rights of their own in traditional African life. Far to the contrary, African marriage is one of his major concerns in several other stories in this collection. In "The Bilal's Fourth Wife," he satirizes Muslim attitudes toward divorce in what is one of his most humorous tales. In "Her Three Days," we have a terribly sympathetic story, depicting a Muslim woman, neglected by her husband who no longer favors her as much as his other wives. The story is one of the harshest attacks on polygamy that we are likely to encounter. In "Letters from France," we have still a third variation on the incompatibility of certain African attitudes toward marriage. The narrator, a young wife of about twenty, writes letters to her girl friend in Africa, relating her shock at discovering that the man her father had arranged for her to marry is seventy-three years old! Yet, Nafi, the young wife, resigns herself to certain inevitable duties from such an arrangement and becomes the mother of the old man's child.

Other stories, and several of his novels, are the direct results of Ousmane's varied personal experiences. "Chaiba the Algerian" tells the story of an African stevedore who works on the docks in Marseilles for twenty-five years. Ousmane's first novel, *Le Docker Noir (The Black Docker)*, was also based on his stevedore experiences. "A Matter of Conscience" in this collection and *Les bouts de bois de Dieu (God's Bits of Wood)*, his finest novel, grew out of Ousmane's experiences as a labor leader. Again, Ousmane's criticism of Africans and Europeans is ubiquitous.

It is probably as a film maker that Sembène Ousmane has become most widely known—both in Africa and in the West. Ousmane has shown a particular dedication to this area in recent years; as his literary output has declined, his films have multiplied (he has made at least half a dozen so far). On a number of occasions, Ousmane has expressed his feelings about films for Africans and the potential of the cinema in Africa. Since so few Africans in his area of the continent can read, he has felt it his duty to work with a media through which he can clearly reach many more Africans than those who can read his novels and short stories. One of his earliest films was based on a short story from this volume, "The Promised Land." (When the film was released in the United States, it was titled *Black Girl*.)

"The Promised Land" is the finest short story in this collection. It is also a story that has been almost completely unappreciated by non-African readers who have often seen it as a melodramatic and stereotypic tale, as little more than a bloody account of an African girl driven to suicide because of the insensitive whites for whom she works. It is that and a great deal more. The whites are totally blind as to what they have forced Diouana to do—to take her own life. (Ousmane's film version makes this even clearer than the short story does.) But the story is, more succinctly, an account of slavery today—modern slavery.

Diouana has come to Paris to continue working for the white family she worked for in Dakar. Full of expectation, seduced by *la belle France*, she comes to discover after three short months that the France she thought about back in Senegal does not exist. She is exploited by the French family; she becomes cook, housekeeper, and nanny to the white children—three full-time positions, a twenty-four-hour work day with no time for herself. Bewildered by France, overworked, isolated because there are no other Africans around (she can't even write letters to her family back in Senegal because she is illiterate), and constantly harassed by the white children who call her names, she finally gives up and slits her wrists in the bathtub. As she thinks, "I've been bought, I do all the work here for three thousand francs [about six dollars a month]. I was enticed here, bound, and now I'm chained here like a slave." Modern slavery—and hardly any more subtle for being that.

The theme of slavery emerges quite early in the story—before Diouana goes to France. An African reader knows that she has been bought, sold at the auction block. Ousmane tells us, "Diouana, looking out of the big window with its wide view of the sea, was mentally following the birds flying high over the vast blue expanse. The offshore island of Gorea was only just visible." She thinks that in France she will be free like the birds flying over the ocean. Yet it is not the bird that comes to represent Diouana's future in France, but the island of Gorea, a few miles off the coast of Dakar—Gorea, the point of departure for millions of slaves, the way station for more African slaves than any other departing point in West Africa. (The slave dungeons still exist on the island today, as a reminder of the horrors of the past. As a tourist visiting the island, standing in one of the dungeons, I felt I could almost hear the breathing of the slaves, shackled to the walls.) How ironic all of this becomes, then, when we continue reading "The Promised Land," going on to the following sentence which states, "She turned her identity card over and over in her hand, looking at it and smiling to herself." Modern slavery; an identity card has replaced the chains.

Diouana's suicide becomes a horrible abomination—irrevocably cutting her off from the cycle of life, yet linking her once again to the thousands of Africans who chose suicide (by jumping overboard into the water from slave ships) rather than enduring slavery in the New World. One has to place suicide in an African context to understand the magnitude of Diouana's final act. By taking her own life, Diouana, who believes in ancestral worship, has severed the chain of being. Her own ancestors will curse her forever, and since she is childless, there will be no descendants on earth to pay homage to her, to pay their respects to her now that she is dead. Diouana has broken one of the strongest taboos of traditional African life. An African reader is repulsed by the end of the story, and only then do the psychological horrors of modern slavery become so apparent. The poem at the end of the story reiterates this theme:

> Diouana,
> Gleam of our coming dawns,
> Like our ancestors, you are victim
> Of barter.

Sembène Ousmane has often walked alone, receiving little recognition for his work. The road he has trod has been a lonely one, because he has often written about things people would rather forget. If the stories in this collection illustrate nothing else, they show that Africans living today are often shackled by some of the same chains that bound their ancestors. Slavery in the past ("Tribal Scars") was not so different from slavery today ("The Promised Land"). One scarred the physical being, the other the soul. Ousmane believes that we need to be aware of these similarities. Let us hope that now that these stories have been translated into English, Sembène Ousmane will find the audience he has long so justly deserved.

Fall 1974   Charles R. Larson
                                          The American University

I

The False Prophet

Mahmoud Fall, with his bronze countenance, aquiline nose and his rapid walk – though not so rapid as the hawk-like glance of his eyes – came of a line of Senegalese Muslims. Faithfully abiding by his ancestors' motto, 'What is mine belongs to me, but there is nothing to stop us sharing what is yours', he did no work. Or to be exact, he did not like killing himself with work. When children slyly asked him, 'Mahmoud, why aren't there any cats where you come from?' he would answer, 'I don't really know.'

It was his way of avoiding saying that cats, like him, liked to be fed without doing anything – which is why there are none to be seen in Upper Senegal. The land there is arid, and the inhabitants erect their tents at nightfall and strike them at dawn. An animal cannot live at man's expense when man is a nomad. Like clings to like, it is said. But these two shun each other. And any cat seen perchance in that country is a pitiful sight.

Mahmoud Fall, tired of doing nothing, with his pockets empty, had decided to journey towards the sunset and the country of the Bilals. In his view these ebony-skinned men were his inferiors, only good for guarding the harem, after having been castrated which eliminates disputes over the paternity of the children.

When he reached Senegal, Mahmoud Fall changed his name. He called himself Aidra, a name which opened all doors to him. He was received everywhere with the respect due to his rank. Having studied the Koran in Mauretania – something that the Senegalese always regard with respect – he profited from his knowledge of the Holy Book, presiding over prayers and sinking into interminable genuflexions. The local people were awestruck; they considered it a very great honour to have a descendant of the noble Aidra as their Imam.

Like his counterpart the cat, Mahmoud arched his back under all these praises. As nature had endowed him with a fine singing voice he was able to delight those around him, making every effort to modulate the syllables before flattening them at the end of each verse. He spent the time between each of the five daily prayers squatting on a sheepskin and telling his beads.

When mealtime came, Mahmoud insisted upon being served apart from the others. The only thanks he gave was to sprinkle children and adults with his abundant spittle. They all rubbed this over their faces, saying 'Amen, amen'. One wonders what Mahmoud thought of all this in the secrecy of his conscience and when he was alone with God.

Being used to moving around, he went from compound to compound and was always received according to the traditional code: 'To each stranger his bowl.' The guest did not refuse anything at first, but as the days went by he became more and more fastidious. According to him, *kuskus* prevented him from sleeping and he complained of indigestion. As his hosts were anxious to remain on the path which leads to Paradise, they cooked special dishes likely to appeal to such a discerning palate as his. But to make certain he did not hesitate at times to go into the kitchen to order what he fancied. That was the brotherly aspect.

Besides being well fed, Mahmoud Fall was amassing small coins, though he never considered there were enough of them for the trouble he was taking. These blacks definitely had a low regard for the value of prayer. And there was another thing – why did they persist in keeping cats? Each time he saw one in a house he felt his hair stand on end, just like the fur of an angry tom-cat. He pulled a face and chased the cat out. Sometimes he preached on the uselessness of cats.

Despite these trifling annoyances, Mahmoud Fall felt that over the months his reputation as a preacher was growing. Learned and holy men everywhere, the talebs, marabouts and tafsirs, had but one phrase on their lips: '*Souma Narr, Souma Narr* (My Moor, My Moor).' Mahmoud secretly thought they were mad. '*Souma Narr!* My Moor. Why *my*? Has anyone ever heard of a black buying a Moor? That would be a topsy-turvy kind of world!'

He wrote more and more signs on pieces of paper for people to carry around with them, and he worked harder than ever to hide his origins and his real aim. To increase his prestige even more, he went so far as to declare that his body was banished from Finahri Dianan – from Hell. And they swallowed that with all the rest.

As the months passed, Mahmoud saw that his hoard was steadily increasing. And one morning, without a word to anyone, he departed as unexpectedly as he had arrived one evening. The elders in their wisdom said, 'If the setting sun brings a stranger, don't look for him at sunrise.'

With his booty in a bag slung over his shoulder, Mahmoud Fall headed briskly towards his beloved Atlas mountains. He walked day and night, with only short rests, thinking of how he would use his capital and taking care to avoid any doubtful encounters. To this end, he made a detour towards the north, which took him through the kingdom of the Tiedes, heathens who worshipped fetishes – though Mahmoud was unaware of this. As he went, he kept congratulating himself: 'Thanks to Satan, I have a great knowledge of the art of appropriating other people's possessions.'

It was the height of the dry season. The sun's rays, like flame-throwers, were setting fire to the sparse tufts of grass; the wind tore at them and flung them towards the far-distant shores, whistling as though to put an end to the unendurable monotony of silence. From the overheated earth there issued a vapour rising to the empty sky. There were the carcasses of animals which had been picked clean at every stage of decomposition and which the wind was gradually burying in the sand. The birds of the air passing uttered cries which were like complaints made to nature. A blend of serenity and unease.

As far as Mahmoud could see, there was no sign of any living being. Only a single tree. A strange tree – strange because of its abundant foliage. The sole survivor in that hell. A tamarind tree.

It was almost the time for prayer. Tired out from his long trek and overcome by the heat, Mahmoud lingered by the tree, wondering whether to pray before or after sleeping. He had to make a decision, and finally he opted for sleep and lay down under the tamarind tree. But what was this? Suddenly he sat up and gave a shout, very loud, although he was alone. 'Hey! Hey! Yes, you up there, come down!'

His words echoed around. Three times he called out, but no reply came. Then he got up, ran to the right and the left, towards the setting sun and to the east. But he was quite alone. There was just him and the tree. An inner voice, doubly suspicious, urged him to bury his treasure. He dug down the length of his forearm; then went to investigate the surroundings, but found nothing. He returned and dug twice as deep, went off again; still nothing. No one at all. He shielded his eyes to peer more clearly into the tree's thick foliage. No one was hiding there. Then he went back to his hole and dug still deeper. This done, he sat down in it and counted his *derhems* which chinked agreeably in the silence. Pleased and reassured, he buried them all, then stretched out to sleep on top of his hoard. But he remembered that he had not paid his due to the Almighty, and addressed Him thus: 'I owe it to you . . .'

After all this performance, sleep was not long in coming to Mahmoud. It was accompanied by a sweet dream in which he was drifting through the desert. As far as the eye could see stretched a vast ocean of sand with interweaving slopes of the dunes. Like ships of this silent sea, camels were plodding along, heads nodding on their long necks; despite the storm that was blowing, the reins were held in position by their brass nose-rings. Grains of sand, harder than steel, pricked through his clothes and stung the skin. Then the dream changed into some sort of reality. Mahmoud Fall saw himself lifted up by a very thin, half-naked black. The man ransacked his hoard, then deliberately proceeded to shave his head.

Mahmoud eventually roused himself, still dazed with sleep, thanked God and yawned.

As a good believer, Mahmoud thought of the first prayer of the day. (If no water is available, sand ablutions are allowed.) He first trickled some sand over his hands and arms to cleanse them of everything unclean he had touched, then sprinkled some over his face and head. In carrying out this ritual he had a shock – he had not felt his mane of hair. He hurriedly put both hands to his head, fingering it all over. He had no hair – his head was bald. Slowly, carefully, making a great effort to control himself, Mahmoud drew his hands down to his chin. His beard had gone too. Wild-eyed and aghast, Mahmoud became aware of something strange happening within him. He thought he could hear voices. And this was so, but they were inner voices.

'It was God who shaved you,' said the first.

'How do you make that out? God doesn't shave anyone.'

Mahmoud, listening to this dialogue, grew livid. The next comment was greeted with a laugh.

'Have faith in God, His mercy is in everything!'

'Ha, ha! You make me laugh. And when you fleeced those poor blighters, in whose name did you do it?'

Mahmoud vigorously shook his head to try to silence these voices, but to no effect; so he put his hands over his ears. He did not want to hear any more. But the voices continued:

'Pray!' one commanded him. 'You have missed two prayers already.'

'Look for your money first,' advised the other. 'Without it, you won't be respected. You won't have any camels. You'll have nothing to eat. Make sure of your money first. It's easier to pray when you're sure of having a full belly.'

Mahmoud obeyed the last injunction. He scrabbled around, casting earth and sand aside so vigorously that his actions were quite unlike those of a normal human being. A goat at bay bites; and Mahmoud would have bitten anyone who tried to stop him looking for his hoard. He was sweating as he crouched there with his tongue hanging out. He could easily have been taken for a giant crab. He pushed the earth away from the hole with his feet. His enveloping *boubou* was half-strangling him, so he wrenched the neck open and then dug down with renewed energy. At last he reached the bottom, and there to his dismay all he found was his sleek, black hair.

He lifted it up, glanced at it in bewilderment, then stared down at the empty hole. Raising his eyes to the tree, he took God as his witness. '*Bilahi-vahali*, this isn't me.'

As he held his hair in one hand and stroked his shaved head with the other, tears welled up in his eyes. '*Bilahi-vahali*, I'm not Mahmoud Fall!' he said again, a sob in his voice.

Then he shouted at the top of his voice, 'My friend, my old friend Mahmoud Fall, come and deliver me from this uncertainty!'

The echo whisked away his call, rolling it over before hurling it on to the plain like a stone on to a galvanized-iron roof. The sound faded into the distance, and he murmured slowly, 'My old friend Mahmoud Fall, don't play this trick on me. I've known you for a long time . . .'

He strained his ears, listening hard, concentrating on a point beyond his range of vision; but he heard nothing. Just a vast emptiness. Then the mocking voices returned.

'Aren't you going to pray?' said the first.

Hardly aware of what he was doing, he stood up, faced towards Mecca, and raised his hands to his temples. '*Allah ackbar!* God is great,' he began.

But his eyes wandered to where his hoard had been hidden.

'Can you still pray when you've been robbed?'

'Ask God who the thief is,' said the other voice.

Mahmoud stood there with his arms raised, not knowing what to do. Then he remembered his dream. 'I wasn't asleep,' he thought.

He had seen the thief; he had even felt that he was being shorn. And the Almighty had not intervened, the Almighty had let it be done.

'No, I'm not going to pray any more,' he said in a low voice, thinking that Allah would not hear him.

Three times he walked round the tree, hoping to find footprints; but in vain. High in the sky, a migrating bird began to sing cheerfully. Mahmoud Fall shouted curses at it. Then he suddenly felt himself to be very much alone.

'On the word of a Moor,' he murmured, 'these sons of slaves are all thieves!'

Rage possessed him, and he ran off like a madman into the desert, his torn *boubou* flapping in the wind. He had just realized that there is no need to believe in Allah in order to be a thief!

2

The Bilal's *Fourth Wife*

He was past middle-age, but despite his years he still had the vigorous bearing of a healthy man. It could hardly be otherwise, for Suliman was the *bilal* of the mosque. He looked after everything – the cleaning, the repairs and maintenance, and the collections in aid of this holy building. As the mosque was timber-built, he had plenty to occupy him. All the faithful admired him and were inclined in his favour; everyone gave alms willingly. Suliman did not expend much energy, so his body became flabby and his face pleasant to look upon. He stifled his laughter, out of piety, and instead smiled at everyone who spoke to him. To sum up, he was an exemplary person, pious and humble – to all appearances at least. A discreet man, certainly . . .

But in private life he was a very different character. He already had three wives, whom he bullied unmercifully because of his vices – and he had quite a few vices, the old humbug! When a young man, Suliman had been in the Sixth Senegalese Rifles, a regiment which served in all the colonial campaigns of the 'twenties – and everyone knows the reputation of that regiment! Sometimes he made two of his wives share his bed. But he never missed the fleeting Holy Hour. He wished to crown his later years with a fourth wife, a young one, about the age of his eldest daughter.

The door of the mosque faced the public fountain, a meeting-place for all the women and girls. After Suliman had whisked round with his broom, he would go and sit outside on his sheepskin and sum up the women. Some of the girls had holes in their bodice, or the low neck was torn, and certain of their movements caused

breasts as firm as unripe fruit to slip into view, the shining flesh
streaked with sweat; at which the other women burst out laughing.

Suliman was on the look-out for such a treat; he sat there like a
sportsman after wild fowl, his eyes reduced to narrow slits and the
tip of his tongue protruding between his lips. He would put a hand
to his throat, stretch his neck and swallow his saliva. His thoughts
ran on the idea of possessing one of these gazelles; and the sight of
all this young flesh made him harsher and more intolerant towards
his old, worn-out wives. The result of it all was that he made their
lives impossible, often beating them.

People (the men) said to them: 'A man like Suliman! There's no
one else so gentle, so calm, so religious as him. You must have
done something, for him to beat you.'

While the wives consoled the one who had been beaten: 'It's a
woman's lot! We have to be patient. Men are our masters under
God. Is there a wife anywhere whose husband has never laid hands
on her?'

Every evening now, the cries of one or other of them could be
heard. But Suliman's taciturn nature acted in his favour.

'They've banded together to make his life intolerable,' men said
between themselves.

'It must be that! Such a good man. Never a word too much and
never a wrong word. If it weren't for him our mosque would be in
ruins.'

'And you never hear him complain,' added another.

To all appearances, Suliman was a martyr to polygamy. This only
served to make men pity and respect him the more. As for him, he
said nothing. But when the women and girls gathered at the fountain, he was in his usual place, sitting on his sheepskin and eyeing
them all. In the evening, after the last prayer, he went round visiting
people. But it was only a pretext, an opportunity to cast an eye over
the girls with their circle of young bloods. In the course of the day
he would call one of the girls and ask her to sweep the courtyard of
the mosque or to fetch water for the ablutions. When they were
alone he would talk a lot of humbug. 'What do the young men say

to you?' he would ask, fastening his eyes on the girl's bosom. 'Be careful of young men . . . my child.'

Sometimes, while pretending to help them, he fumbled at their clothing and pawed them. The youngsters paid no attention, knowing he was old enough to be their father. At such times, at the height of his perverse pleasure, his mouth fell open, his eyes turned upwards and he broke into a sweat. Becoming more emboldened, he fell upon one of them . . .

The girls dared not complain to anyone. Who would believe them? Such a pious man! And who had three wives . . . The victims had to say nothing or defend themselves. Meanwhile Suliman knocked his wives about for anything and everything. Having whetted his appetite with some of the girls, he began to neglect his duties as *bilal*; all except one – taking the collections. For that, he never missed an opportunity, not a single prayer. But the mosque began to fall into disrepair.

In the space of a year, Suliman had become a different man; with increasing age, he was consumed with an insatiable lust. He was like a camel on heat, except that he did not foam at the mouth. But he was still neatly dressed, and was even more polite than usual. There was a lot of talk about him, for the change in him affected all the faithful.

'His wives make his life a misery. We must do something about it,' said one man.

'Ought we to find him a fourth wife?'

'That's it. We must find him another wife, one who'll make up for all the beastliness of the others.'

'Yes, for if it weren't for Suliman, we shouldn't have a mosque at all. The other districts all have fine mosques. A year ago, ours used to be the best kept and the cleanest. Suliman isn't that old – he can still keep a girl satisfied all night.'

'But where shall we find her? A girl who will show up the other three wives and who doesn't live around here. For they're all of one mind here, the women all stick together.'

'Then let each of us look around among his acquaintances.'

The weeks went by. The *bilal* got wind of the elders' deliberations, but made no attempt to limit his indulgences; every morning he sent for a girl and satisfied himself.

Eventually they found Yacine N'Doye. She came of a fisherman's family and was not like other girls. She was almost twenty – and what a tongue she had! No man had come to ask for her; she was a tomboy, a hard worker, and joined in the young men's games and competitions, challenging them. And when her father told her that he had found her a husband, she did not quibble, although she would have liked to ask a few questions.

One evening Suliman was seen to go into the house. Yacine's father was very flattered. It was a great honour to know that his daughter could please the *bilal*. And Suliman, a prey to his desires, was not niggardly. 'If you want the heifer you must take care of the cow.' He was generous in helping his future father-in-law; and at the mosque he pretended not to see him at collection time, or else he gave him his coins back when they were alone.

One Friday, Yacine was betrothed to him. There was a great feast; a sheep was slaughtered, and all the faithful took part in the festivities. Suliman promised in front of everyone that he would slaughter two bulls for Yacine's virginity.

During the months which elapsed between the betrothal and the wedding night, Suliman seemed a new man. Everyone was sure that Yacine was 'intact', as pure as spring water. The sole subject of gossip was the coming celebrations. Yacine's father, her mother and all her relations, near and distant, plied her with questions.

'But how do you expect me to get on with that old man?' she asked them.

'That old man? He's giving you what the young ones haven't got. Honour, rank, esteem – to say nothing of two bulls on your wedding day! Even your mother didn't have that.'

Then there were the little presents of toiletry, fibre trunks, head-scarves, waist-cloths and bracelets. And despite his age, Suliman

decided to build a new hut for Yacine. 'Everything must be new
for a virgin!' he told the other men.

The date for her 'induction' was postponed. Suliman controlled
his impatience. The hut was not quite ready. 'Everything in it is
Yacine's. I give it all to her,' he said boastfully.

'Suliman, there's no one like you,' said the men.

The day came when Yacine entered into her new home. The
following day, a white waist-cloth stained with blood was passed
round by the women, from compound to compound, to general
rejoicing. This made the bride's parents very proud; their honour
was safe. For the whole of that week, everyone ate nothing but meat.
Drums beat, and the girls organized dances in the evenings.

Everything gradually returned to normal. Yacine was the favoured
wife. But at the end of three years, when Yacine was only twenty-
three, she had had just one child. She had become a woman, with
all a woman's qualities and faults. (In this climate of perpetual
spring, passions run deep and fast. A man on the decline cannot
hope to satisfy a woman in her prime.) While Yacine's vigour was
mounting, Suliman's was diminishing. Night after night, as nothing
was forthcoming, Yacine stayed awake. She regretted having had
her sensuality aroused. Suliman was still granting three days of his
presence to each of his wives. The old ones, broad in the beam
and worn out from successive pregnancies, were not particularly interested in 'that'. Once a month was quite enough for
them. But Yacine had only the one child; and she ought to be
breeding.

One day Yacine went to see her parents. She had this serious
problem on her mind.

'Father, I want to come back home.'

'Why?'

'Well, I'm afraid I'm not getting on with my husband.'

'And why not?' he asked again, looking straight at her.

Modesty prevented her from entering into explanations. She
dropped her eyes and turned to leave again.

'Just remember, daughter, that Suliman has spent an enormous amount, and if you leave him for no reason – that is, for no valid reason – I shall have to pay him back . . . and I can't.'

Yacine, unable to bear the frustration any longer, took a lover, none other than Suliman's nephew. One morning, having spent three nights with his third wife, Suliman went to Yacine's hut. He found his nephew in bed with her. He said nothing. The lovers had seen him too. 'You get sick of what is disagreeable; what is agreeable makes you enterprising.'

In the days that followed, Suliman said nothing about it to anybody; nor did Yacine or the nephew. It was a secret between them. 'If you repudiate your wife, you lose the dowry. And for such a reason, witnesses are necessary.' Keeping the secret was even worse! It poisoned his thoughts. The mere knowledge that another man had taken his place was enough to age Suliman; and in the space of six weeks he lost his fine bearing and became consumed with jealousy.

'Are you ill, *bilal*?' the faithful asked him, seeing him wasting away.

'What, me? Good heavens, no! Nothing serious, it'll soon go.'

In Suliman's house a tragi-comedy was being enacted by three silent players, with no spectators but themselves. Yacine could not quit Suliman without refunding all the expense he had gone to on her account. Her father was in no position to return the money if she were declared the guilty party in a divorce. Both husband and wife stuck to their respective positions. Suliman thought 'If she returns to her father's house, I shall get my money back and be able to keep my son.' While Yacine said to herself 'If I go back home, I shall have to return everything to him.' Then she thought 'But why should I? I didn't ask him for anything. If I leave him, it's because he isn't a man any more.'

Yacine, meanwhile, had no embarrassment over spending her time pleasantly with her lover. While Suliman, ailing from a disorder that was undermining his prestige and his dignity, quarrelled with his other wives. Once again the men said, 'Poor fellow, he's venting his wrath on dead donkeys.'

Another year went by, and Yacine was pregnant again. When the baby was born, the elders, acting through loyalty or hypocrisy, made preparations to baptize the child. But Suliman, with a final spark of honesty, objected.

'I'm not going to baptize a child which isn't mine,' he said.

'Well, we know that. It is the will of God. This child is yours because Yacine is your wife.'

'What will of God? God has nothing to do with it.'

Yacine had not waited for the outcome; she had returned to her parents' taking everything with her, even the broom. She had just appropriated everything Suliman had ever given her. (It must be remembered that in a case like this, the wife in fact has to return everything.) The *bilal* was to some extent pleased by Yacine's action, for he thought that he could start divorce proceedings and get all his property back. In fact he was very cheerful about it. But he made no move to see his parents-in-law. On the contrary, it was Yacine's father who approached the *bilal* at the mosque, after prayers, hoping that the latter would raise the matter. But the cunning Suliman diverted the conversation to religious subjects.

The couple apparently had no intention of taking their case for dispute before the elders. However, people gossiped, and eventually there was a meeting to discuss it. Suliman finally made up his mind to plead his case before the gathering of elders.

'I will grant her the divorce, but first she must pay back all my expenses and return my child to me.'

(He had right on his side, by local law and custom.)

'There are two children,' was the reply. 'Both are yours. Besides, you haven't told us why she left you.'

'Oh, she can tell you that.'

'Well, that's very true. She was the one who went away. She must have her reasons, which you may know nothing about.'

They questioned Yacine's father. 'So she wants to divorce him?'

'She says not.'

The elders were astonished. 'She says not?'

This confused the whole affair beyond comprehension. When the dust had blown away, they would see more clearly, said the elders philosophically. That evening they sent for Yacine.

'Yacine, you must go back to your husband.'

'I tell you I will not.'

'Very well, so you are bringing a suit for divorce. The sole fact that you are no longer happy with your husband means that you will be granted a divorce. Then you will have to pay back —'

'In the first place,' retorted Yacine, 'I am not asking for a divorce. In the second place, I just can't go on living with him. Thirdly, I've nothing to give back – and the child is not his.'

The elders, wise men though they were, had to admit that they were baffled by this. Suliman was evidently right; the matter could not be settled among themselves. It was taken to the Cadi.

The most learned men from all around were called in. A delegation was even sent to ask the great Froh-Toll to attend, the man whose truths smarted like a squirt of lemon-juice in the eye. The court-house could hold only fifty people, so it was decided that the case should be heard in the open air. Many idlers took up places on the village square the day before the case was due to start. The marabouts consulted the Holy Book of Koranic laws and reviewed the *Farata* and the *Sounna*, the rules and customs governing the union and separation of man and wife.

The time came, the case was opened by the *Hali*, the judge, who called upon 'anyone who can throw light on this matter' to do so. Then he addressed the contestants.

'Suliman, will you agree to take back your wife and your children? And you, Yacine, are you prepared to go back to your husband with his children? We will hear what you have to say.'

'Yacine left me,' replied Suliman. 'I want her to pay back all my expenses and give me my child.'

'So you don't want your wife, Suliman?' said the Hali.

'If a wife leaves her husband's house and takes everything with her, it means that she has no intention of returning.'

'To all appearances, that is true,' put in Froh-Toll. 'What do you say to that, Yacine?'

'I say that I have not divorced Suliman. He was my husband, but later he was no longer capable of being my husband. That is why I left him.'

'That is what you say. But only Suliman can set you free,' said the Hali.

'It is not the same thing as leaving her husband's home,' commented Froh-Toll.

'She left me and she must pay me back,' said Suliman.

'I have nothing to pay back,' retorted Yacine.

'Yacine, according to the rules and customs which united the two of you, you must give back the dowry.'

'Very well, if you think that's fair. But I will only agree on condition that Suliman gives me back my virginity.'

That was not written in the rules and customs, but it aroused much controversy. Some, especially the young ones, supported Yacine. But the elders failed to see the logic of it and took a different view of her case. Realizing that here was a moot point, the Hali called for silence and went on to consider the question of the children.

'There are two children, and as Yacine has broken the marriage contract, as we now know, the custody of the children devolves on their father, Suliman.'

'I should like to add . . . or rather clear up a small matter. The second child is not mine,' Suliman stated for all to hear.

'I shan't give him or anything up,' retorted Yacine.

Until then, most of those present had supported Yacine, but they did not agree with her about the custody of the child. Everyone recognized the father's sacred right to have possession of his offspring – everyone except Froh-Toll.

'I should like to put a few questions to you, the wise men,' began Froh-Toll. 'It appears that the child should be returned to the father. But are we sure that a child should be returned to its father by right of birth?'

'Oh yes. It says so in the Holy Book.'

Froh-Toll was thoughtful for a few moments, then he said

composedly: 'I myself, here before you, I lost my father when I had been in my mother's womb for only two months. The death of my father did not prevent me from coming into the world . . .'

'The death of a husband will never prevent his pregnant wife from giving birth,' stated the Hali.

'But now consider that the contrary had happened, that my mother had died when two months' pregnant. Should I be alive now?'

'No, no,' shouted the crowd.

'So by what right does Suliman demand the custody of the child? There can always be doubt as to who is the father of a child. But never as to who is the mother.'

3
In the Face of History

'If you see that film, you'll never in your life be able to trust a woman again,' said one of the three men.

They were standing outside the Mali Cinema in the teeming district of Rebeuse. All three looked along the queue of men, women and children which was growing every minute; beyond the cinema lights, darkness came down like a curtain. On the fringe of the bright halo was a row of food-stalls; prostitutes were strolling up and down in the cool air, for it was not so stifling as the evening before. Now and again a breeze wafted a sickening stench of rotting garbage from the houses.

The smallest man of the three, the one in the middle, looked thoughtfully at the cinema poster again and then announced, 'I've seen that film,' and he read out syllable by syllable, 'Sam-son and De-li-lah.'

'Well, shall we go home or what? I've seen it, too,' added the third, automatically lifting his tunic and putting his hand into the pocket of his baggy trousers. He gazed at the crowd again.

Just then a taxi drew up at the entrance to the cinema. The man nudged the other two and nodded towards the new arrivals. A couple dressed in European clothes had got out of the taxi. The man was wearing a Terylene suit with a sharp crease to the trousers; his shoes shone in the darkness, his nylon shirt had lost its creamy colour, and he had a dark tie. He looked all round him like someone used to weighing up a crowd, and his eyes were gloomy. He gave a sniff of distaste, paid the taxi-driver and turned round again. The woman seemed young but her face gave no clue to her age; she had bare shoulders – shoulders of distinction, like her whole appearance – and a white silk-and-wool shawl was draped carelessly round them. The crinkle had been taken out of her hair, which she wore in a bouffant style; rings dangled from her ears, and her bell-shaped skirt was knee-length.

'I know that fellow – it's Abdoulaye,' said one of the three. 'He's a primary school teacher. And the girl's his wife. She's called Sakinetou. She's got a Technical College certificate. For their wedding, eight oxen and sixteen sheep were killed, and no end of money was given away. They come from round our way – at least, the man grew up in the same district as I did'.

He ended his commentary as the couple drew near.

When they had passed, the delicate, pleasing fragrance of the woman lingered in the air. The three turned to look at her.

'What's showing?' the man said in French, in a reluctant tone, and he read out, 'Samson and Delilah'.

'Yes,' she answered, and half-turned towards the crowd. Her eyes met those of the man who had spoken, and he gave her a broad beam of recognition. Sakinetou's face hardened.

'It's a silly film,' Abdoulaye was saying. 'I've seen it. We'd do better to go somewhere else.'

'Where else?' the woman put in. Her eyes were glittering with anger.

A man whose clothes gave him a stately appearance, one large *boubou* over another, stalked between the couple, followed by his two wives and five small boys.

'What's the film, uncle [meaning "dear"]?' asked the wife immediately behind him.

'I don't know. We shall find out when we get inside. Be careful not to lose the children.'

'I hope there's some singing in it,' said the second wife just as she came abreast of the Technical College certificate-holder.

'In this cinema they only put on Arab or Indian films,' said the man in the voluminous garments.

'Well?' asked Abdoulaye when the family procession had passed.

'Well, I'm not going anywhere else. It's been like this for months. You don't like going to dances, and I want to see this film. And you make yourself out to be a teacher. This Saturday I don't want to waste my time with your pals who do nothing but talk about their game of cards,' said the woman aggressively.

'We might go and see the African Ballet at the Youth Club. It isn't far from here.'

'Oh, you and your passion for the theatre! That's for the whites,' she retorted (and again her eyes caught the look of the one of the three who knew them and who was losing nothing of their argument). 'Shall we get the tickets?'

'Me, d'you mean? No,' said Abdoulaye, looking stern. Then he quickly asked, 'What shall we do?'

From somewhere came an uproar that continued, booming over all their heads, to which was added the shrilling of whistles. People in the queue began pushing and jostling. Two shafts of light swept the black night above the sea.

'Samson and Delilah,' Abdoulaye read it again, wavering. Then he added, 'But you've already seen it.'

'Yes, I know. But I don't want to stay at home on a Saturday. I want to go out and enjoy myself.'

'We could go to the Ballet . . .'

'Oh, the Ballet!' she exclaimed markedly, with a slight tone of defiance. 'I want to see "Samson and Delilah".'

'And I don't . . .'

'I do.'

They glared at each other again, and she went on in the same defiant tone: 'I'm not an illiterate *fatou*. I can pay for myself.' She swung round, and saw the three men staring at her. 'Stupid lot,' she muttered, and walked briskly towards the ticket-office; then changed her mind and came back. Abdoulaye had not moved; but he too was getting angry.

'I'm off. I'm going to see my father,' she said.

'Anyway, you've got to queue for tickets. We'd miss the start of the film.' He was beginning to have enough of this struggle.

'I'm not going there now . . .' She stepped towards the roadway and hailed a passing taxi. The sound of its engine faded into the distance.

Left to himself, Abdoulaye stared again at the poster with its large lettering: 'Tonight, Samson and Delilah. An historical film.' Then he lit a cigarette and made off into the night.

'What was all that about?' said one of the three wonderingly.

'What was it about? Oh, it's all over between them. They've lost their sense of balance.'

'Just like this country . . . No balance left . . . Shall we go and see the film?'

'Suppose we went to see the Toucoleur *kora*-player? It would be a bit of a change.'

'Changing your country or your wife doesn't solve any problems. If everyone thought like that . . . I wonder what Abdoulaye will do?'

'Well, shall we go home or not?' the other asked again.

They all looked at the poster. Then with one accord all three started to whistle the Soundiata tune, and walked away.

4
Love in Sandy Lane

It had no street sign, but everyone knew it as Sandy Lane. It was short – no more than two hundred yards long – and started at the charming villa 'Mariame Ba', which blocked the far end, and came out on to the main street which ran right through the district.

It had got its name from a great number of things.

Opposite the entrance to Sandy Lane the villa 'Mariame Ba' stood proud and spruce, painted yellow and blue. Amid the collection of decrepit old shacks, it had a manorial aspect; its greyish windows disclosed three rooms, each covered from floor to ceiling with photographs, some in glass frames. After *timis*, the sunset prayer, El Hadj Mar usually climbed on to the terrace overlooking the street. Below him was spread the jumble of rooftops, some flat, some pointed, the straw huts and the shacks. The inhabitants of Sandy Lane might have seemed very proud of 'their villa'. But deep down, each of them nursed a feeling of animosity towards the old employee of the late colonial administration, who from his lofty perch openly pried on their every action.

First in the lane, going down on the right, was Pourogne's shack, which leaned outwards and was shored up by three beams firmly embedded in the sand; the bottom planks were crumbling away and had been patched up with pieces of galvanized iron, and the red paint had faded in the sun. Then came the public fountain which had been condemned. (It was whispered in the district that this was due to the inhabitants' obstinacy towards government policy; for

everyone except El Hadj Mar, so it was said, had voted 'No' in the
1958 referendum.* So because of their rebellious character they
were obliged to go elsewhere for water.) Next came Yaye Hady's
compound, which was fenced round with bamboo wattle; in order
to be considered a member of the Sandy Lane community, Yaye
Hady had blocked up the old entrance giving on to the main street
and had made a new one on the Sandy Lane side. Adjacent to him
was the Niangs' *M'bar*. The Niang family still carried on the gold-
smith's craft handed down to them by their forbears, and by their
love of this delicate work had greatly contributed to the fame of the
lane. Their female clientele came from all parts of the town. The
eldest Niang, a big fellow with a large behind, had a jolly face and
the cavernous eyes of the old, without eyebrows or lashes; he sat
outside his workshop and gave interminable *salamalecs* to everyone
coming out into the lane, except to El Hadj Mar. Then there was
Salif's carpenter's shop; he was a wiry, very dark man, most amusing
when so inclined, but a tireless singer. The people of Sandy Lane
became worried if he was silent. That is why, when Salif's voice was
no longer heard, it was said that 'the Sandy Lane people' were in
a bad way. And last of all on the right-hand side, adjoining the
villa 'Mariame Ba', was the big shack housing the family of old
Maissa. He was a very devout man who never went out without
his beads.

On the left-hand side of the lane was the mother-house of Granny
Aita; the brick base was crumbling away and was riddled with holes
into which the hens and ducks vanished. Three tall, pliable *filos*
served as a refuge for the *catiocatios*. As soon as it was dusk, these
weaver-birds filled the air with their 'catio-catio' calls, hence their
name. Their textile-nests looked like dangling black balls in the
gathering darkness. Next came Mavdo's patch; he was the charcoal
merchant, and a black dune as high as a hut spilled over from the
patch. Then came the Youth Club, a hut with 'Palais de l'ONU'
(UNO Palace) chalked above the door. A few dozen young men

* Whether or not to become independent of France. (Tr.)

met there, most of them out of work through no fault of their own. Through the door could be seen piles of old magazines, emblems of many nations and pictures of Heads of State and leaders of political parties all over the world. When the young men were tired of discussions they drowned their passion for politics in Moorish tea. Last of all, at an angle to the villa 'Mariame Ba', was an unfinished building intended long ago for a policeman. When evening came, children went and relieved themselves among the heaps of bricks still lying around, as though it was the most natural thing in the world.

Such was the outward appearance, the material aspect, of Sandy Lane. It was nothing to write home about. But the people who lived there harboured a different kind of wealth, which had brought renown to this part of the town.

Once a week all the housewives got together to clean the lane. Early in the morning they all lined up in front of their doorways on both sides of the lane; they would bend down, little brush in hand, as though about to begin a dance. The two lines advanced and met in the middle, where, as if working to music, they divided into little groups and swept towards the main street like rippling waves. Then they dug a hole and buried all the rubbish. The lane was made of very fine sand which did not crunch underfoot. It was because of this rather exaggerated cleanliness that the inhabitants proudly allowed people from neighbouring streets to organize drum sessions in their lane, and the faithful there celebrated the birth of the Prophet.

It was a peaceful little lane, and the only one in the town to have such diverse and yet united characters living in it. However, a very common incident, too common at the present time, put an end to this state of affairs . . . The people of Sandy Lane were not scandalmongers, but – and this was the cause of the trouble – neither did they confide in one another.

In Sandy Lane there lived a girl, Kine, who was El Hadj Mar's eldest daughter by his second wife. Her beauty was talked about all over the town. Her physical charms were a favourite subject for the songs of the youths who frequented the 'Palais de l'ONU'. When she returned from market, her calabash on her slightly tilted head, her graceful neck curved a little and her smooth, velvety shoulders showing above the wide neck of her muslin *boubou*, her walk so stately, the people of Sandy Lane – especially the men – turned and teased her; and she smiled back, showing her regular little white teeth.

Nothing was a secret in Sandy Lane; but no one ever talked of it, that was all. Everyone knew that Kine's heart beat only for Yoro, the old charcoal-merchant's son. Yoro was a shy young man, but he also played the kora. Sometimes he left the shelter of the 'Palais de l'ONU' and plucked up his courage to go and strum his kora beneath the windows of the villa 'Mariame Ba'. When he and Kine happened to come face to face, or when their eyes met, there was a pleasant rush of blood, a warm, sweet rush of blood, in both of them; it rose from their toes and ran through their veins, giving them a warm sensation, warmer than anything else.

The people of Sandy Lane were simple or naïve and they liked these two youngsters; and as this love reminded them of their own, they seemed to bless it by a conspiratorial silence. They thought quite simply that if two people loved one another, nothing could be strong enough to stand in their way.

Secretly – though the Sandy Lane folk were not very talkative – they were preparing to celebrate the wedding in their own fashion. All of them, men and women, said to Kine whenever she passed by, 'How's Yoro?'

And to Yoro they said, 'How's Kine?'

When Yoro came home from work at midday and at six o'clock, as soon as he reached Pourogne's shop he would look towards the villa. He scanned all the windows; and Kine, knowing it was the time for him to return, would be standing at one of the windows. And all Sandy Lane having discovered the young couple's secret, their way of greeting and communicating with each other, as soon

B

as Yoro entered the lane a swarm of eyes instantly turned in the direction of the villa. They were very discreet, though, the lane's inhabitants. They never said very much. In the end the two turtle-doves gave up this deaf-and-dumb language; and in the evenings, after the last prayer, when everybody had come to sit outside and the night was draped in its starry robe, Yoro would sit in a fold of darkness and strum his kora while Kine, sitting with her parents in front of the villa, would let her thoughts run on.

Sandy Lane was well known. It was often mentioned in the songs of griots, for El Hadj Mar, a generous man, frequently invited story-tellers into his house. The tale of the mute love of Kine and Yoro went from mouth to mouth. Yet neither of them had gone beyond stealing shy glances, blinking, or sounding the quivering notes of the kora.

One day people saw mature men who occupied prominent positions in the country arriving in Sandy Lane. Among them was more than one Minister, several Chief Secretaries and other personalities. They all went to El Hadj Mar's house, where they spent the whole day feasting and drinking to excess. And they returned several times. Every week holes were dug in front of the villa and soon whole sheep could be seen roasting on spits over a wood fire. There were always official cars parked at the entrance to Sandy Lane; big, luxurious cars.

The regulars of the 'Palais de l'ONU' felt frustrated; they supported Yoro. The other people, experienced observers as they were, muttered indignantly. Every day now, at midday and at six, their eyes remained firmly fixed on the ground; and the strumming of the kora was no longer heard in the evening. A month went by, a funereal silence settled on the lane – and Yoro had disappeared. Three months later, Kine was seen no more. (I was told that after the disappearance of the lovers, two trees were planted – a male and a female.) But since these happenings, Sandy Lane has ceased to be the pride of the district; the rubbish piles up, and the women throw their slops outside the villa 'Mariame Ba'. These people who formerly never uttered an oath have become foul-mouthed. The young men leave to live elsewhere. No longer are religious chants heard in the lane, and the drums throb no more . . .

Sandy Lane has become the saddest place in the world.

And as I walked around Dakar I wondered if the whole town was not under this curse.

5

A Matter of Conscience

The two windows overlooking the Rue de Thiong were open, but those on the Rue Blanchot side were shuttered against the pulsating heat of the sun. In the Trade Union office that afternoon, Ibra, a thickset, very dark man with close-cropped hair going grey at the temples, a talkative fellow, was perched on the edge of the table and holding forth. The office workers were listening – three of them, sitting on a bench; the middle one was smiling stupidly, showing teeth worn away by too much chewing of kola-nuts.

'I went to see her last night,' Ibra was recounting. 'She's a very nice girl. And what d'you think? I found some scum there! A lot of layabouts – never done a day's work in their lives! I summed them up at a glance, and also saw that the bed – the only place worthy of a buck like me – was occupied (you don't get an old hand like me acting the prude). So I said to the girl, "Sister, I'm off." She came outside with me. So guess what? I took her off to her aunt's! For I've got a trump card up there in the citadel. When we got to her aunt's, I said to her, "Well, sister, didn't you get my message, that I should be coming to see you?"'

'"Yes, I did," she answered, and went on, "but brother, I couldn't send them away just like that. You don't swop over without knowing what you're getting in exchange, do you?"

'Right, I thought to myself, now I know where I am. And I laid down my conditions. "Do you want me? If so, I don't expect anyone else to be at your place but me, understand? Either it's me, and only me, or not me at all."'

'A man of action,' commented one of the men on the bench.

Flattered by this, Ibra stuck his chest out, swinging his stubby legs. He continued with his tale, determined to tell all of his exploit of the evening before.

'After a few seconds' hesitation, she replied, "If that's what you want, I'll tell them never to set foot here again."

'"Yes, that's what I want," I said. "Now you know who is responsible for you. Your slightest desires will be satisfied by me alone." Her aunt gave up her bedroom to us, and we stayed there until three in the morning. As for the others, I don't know what happened to them. Before leaving her I laid down three five-thousand-franc notes . . .'

'Fifteen thousand!' exclaimed one of the others. 'And it's only the nineteenth of the month. Only a Member of Parliament could do that. It's a lot of money . . . on the nineteenth of the month.'

'Oh, I'll do more than that for her.'

'She'll be like a third wife?' suggested the man with bad teeth.

'Not likely! Still, I think she's all right.'

'Until you get her in the family way, then you'll drop her,' said the other official, looking up at Ibra.

'We'll baptize her,' smiled Ibra.

Ibra was the great hope of the working class. He had been one of the most impassioned of those who had stormed the colonial fortress to obtain for the blacks equal wages with the whites. Then in the course of time had come Independence. He had known the worst hardships of that period. His followers had constantly increased until there came a time when he stood for election to the National Assembly. He had got in (and he was still a member). Then things had changed completely; those who previously slammed the door in his face now welcomed him, and the big bosses were delighted to see him at every reception. He acquired a villa and a car without paying out a penny; and he had a bank account which, it is true, was not increased by many dividends, yet small sums accumulated in it as he worked overtime by attending meetings of boards of directors. He spent his holidays in France. He had an office at the Trades Union Council.

Malic came in. 'Hello, everybody,' he said, shaking the hands held out to him. He was a young man with an emaciated face, narrow, deep-set eyes and a determined chin with a little beard.

'Everything all right with you?' asked Ibra, still perched on the table.

'No.'

'How's that?'

'How's that!' exclaimed Malic indignantly, looking angry. 'Last week I sent a report on our situation to this office. Workers are being laid off and the others are expected to do overtime without an increase in rates.'

Malic turned to the pen-pusher on his right, who said quickly, 'I gave him the report.'

'Ah yes,' admitted Ibra. 'It's here. All right, I'll have a look at it.'

'But the boss is standing them off tonight. There's no time to lose. It's the old hands who are being dismissed – those with fifteen to twenty years' service. And it's doubtful if they'll get their pay in lieu of notice. We want to know what the T.U.C. thinks about it – and you're our representative. Because we've decided –'

'Decided what?' demanded Ibra, lifting his head and narrowing his ferrety eyes. His flat face became congested. 'In the first place, I don't like ultimatums,' he exclaimed, getting off the table. 'You assume too much. I was leading workers' movements before you even started working. If union members have better conditions now, it's thanks to me. You think that all there is to do is to decide, just like that? I haven't read your paper. I'm overwhelmed with work because of this break-up of the Federation (Federation of Mali – the Sudan and Senegal).'

'It's in your drawer there. You've had that report for a week now,' said Malic, starting to go round the table towards the drawer.

Ibra held him back. 'There's nothing here belonging to you. This is *my* office. Of course I'm not blind to the labour situation. Are you or I or the bosses responsible for what's happening now? No, it's this Mali trouble! The railway line has been cut, so it's only to be expected that factories should reduce their labour force, especially yours where the output is all exported to the Sudan. You see, I know the situation better than you do!'

'So you're suggesting it's the fault of the Sudanese? You yourself sent a declaration in the name of all the workers to say that we support the government's action. That was done without consulting any of the unions. And that –'

'I can see –'

'Let me finish,' exclaimed Malic. (Some workers and idlers were gathering below the open windows overlooking the Rue de Thiong.) 'There's a lack of integrity in the way you carry out your functions. It was the same at the time of Guinea's independence, when workers were being laid off.'

'Look here, Malic!' shouted Ibra. 'I'm not taking orders from any of your lot! And if you start any subversive tricks you'll soon find out where you are and who you're up against, understand? Here, the whole country is behind the government . . .'

'And I'm telling you it's not true! The country is still in the hands of colonialists. You and your lot just carry out orders!'

'I've nothing more to say to you,' snapped Ibra.

The two stood glaring at each other.

'I'm going back to see the workers,' declared Malic. 'You're all witnesses,' he added as he went out.

A few minutes later, Ibra left the office too. His new black Peugeot was waiting, and he was driven to the Ministry of Labour. Later his car was seen on the Bel-Air road. Meanwhile the workers had assembled in the factory yard. Ibra arrived and went to see the factory manager. When he came out he said nothing to the waiting men, merely calling a meeting for the following afternoon at the union offices.

When he arrived home – to an expensively furnished villa with three air-conditioners and surrounded by a green hedge – he reflected on the material benefits he had acquired and made a mental inventory of his possessions: three houses bringing in good rents, two taxis; and every day he could eat his fill. Thinking this over, he realized that nothing now bound him to the needy.

At three o'clock next afternoon there were some fifty men gathered in the courtyard of the Trade Union building. Ibra addressed them, with the Minister of Labour and Planning, the factory manager and a few officials standing by his side.

'I saw your manager yesterday. He received me in a very friendly manner, and we reached agreement on a number of points. I know it's very hard when the head of a family is without work. But you must realize that your manager is not responsible for the present situation – which concerns us all. The troubles in the Mali Federation have serious consequences for all of us. You heard what the President of the Republic said about the situation the other day . . . Well! The Minister of Labour, here beside me, promises that you will be taken on again as soon as things get back to normal. Moreover, your wages in lieu of notice will be duly paid. Don't join the nation's enemies and don't listen to them, those public moaners who say that the present state of affairs is due to the slackness of the present government. We're independent – as independent as any other country! We don't want a new colonialism here, a coloured one, more cruel and abject than the other. One more word before I finish. Malic has been a bad delegate. He should have given a monthly report to me and to the union committee. The Minister and I are sure that if we had been warned in time we could have seen that fewer men were laid off work. But –'

'I object! That's not true!' cried Malic. 'I've sent in a report every month. Only yesterday, after leaving you, I came here. The staff can tell you so.'

Malic ran across to the office. The door was locked.

'There's no one in my office. I've always worked by myself.'

'Comrades, I ask you to tell the truth. Have I ever once failed to carry out my duties to you?'

'I haven't told you everything,' added Ibra. 'The manager told me that Malic asked for certain benefits for himself.'

'You see how you were acting on your own,' put in the manager. 'I've been very good to my workmen. I've let them have a truck to take them home at midday and bring them back at two o'clock.'

'But –,' began Malic.

'That's enough!' broke in the Minister. (Malic was staring hard at Ibra.) 'We know you, Malic. Subversion only leads to prison. What your deputy and representative with the government has just told you is true. Your motion of support in the longest night in our history will remain an everlasting pledge. On behalf of the government, I thank you. Tomorrow, you will receive what is due to you, and in a few weeks you will be back at work. And now, I hope you will excuse me; I have a great deal of work to do.'

The Minister, followed by his henchmen and the factory manager, went away.

Ibra avoided any discussion with Malic. He asked two men to go with him somewhere or other, and left.

Malic was walking away when a dozen or so of the men went up to him. 'You were quite right just now, Malic,' said their spokesman, the oldest factory worker. 'But you see, you must see, we hadn't the courage to back you up. Yes, it was courage that was lacking. Those types have nothing in common with us! They're black outside – but inside they're just like the colonialists.'

6
The Mother

I have told you about kings and their ways of living; not all, by any means, but some of them. They succeeded each other from father to son, and the heir apparent was given a special education. Griots sang him the praises of his ancestors, their doings and exploits. Once crowned, an absolute ruler owing allegiance to no one, he became a tyrant (though not always). His attendants carried spittoons of chased silver, real works of art, or ceremonial pipes – some more than six feet long – that had bowls carved in the shape of human heads. Other attendants constantly waved fans made of ostrich and peacock feathers of rare colours. There were still others to sing his praises and to dance for his entertainment. All cherished a desire to see him burnt alive, for he was not a God but a despot with the power of life or death over his subjects. It was not unusual for him to condemn to death someone he thought to be lacking in enthusiasm for his particular task.

Fate strikes at those who tempt it! A law can be said to be just when it is made by the people. Now the king decreed that 'no man shall marry a girl unless He be the first to spend the night with her'. A wicked law, of course. But no one opposes an absolute monarch.

He committed so many base actions that his ministers complained to the oracles, but all in vain. Their daughters submitted to the ruling when the time came; none dared to elude the obligation. The common people were resigned. All was going well for the king. Then one day a man whose origins no one knew came to marry the king's daughter. 'Is he going to do the same with her?' everyone wondered. But that same evening the king repealed the accursed law.

For a time, all was well. The king appeared to calm down; but he was only biding his time in order to indulge his tastes. Deep within him was a smouldering anger. 'The elders have raised a dam against my pleasure,' he said to himself.

For many days messengers scoured the outlying districts under his authority, announcing that the king wanted to see all his subjects, the sick and the infirm included, under penalty of having all their goods confiscated. When everyone in the kingdom was present, he gave orders to kill all men over the age of fifty. As soon as he had spoken, the deed was accomplished. The earth became stained with blood. The sun dried up the blood, the wind blew over it and licked it, and bare feet obliterated the last traces; but the passage of time did not wipe out the memory in the minds of men . . .

Nobody dared defy this madman. He indulged his vices more than ever, taking not only girls about to be married but all who had reached marriageable age. Only a few mothers succeeded in preserving their daughters from this maniac's sadistic lust.

(*Glory to thee, woman, boundless ocean of tenderness, blessed art thou by thy flow of gentleness.*)

The king, drunk but still not sated, journeyed in quest of fresh maidens. In his chief town no one was left who took his fancy. At the entrance to a village he halted for a drink, and then his surprise was so great that for a moment it quenched his thirst. He gave orders for the girl who had brought him the drink to be carried off. She was beautiful. On hearing her cries, her mother came running. (What could a woman do against servants six feet tall?) Nevertheless their strong arms failed to control her. A blow sent her to the ground. She was on her feet again in a moment, and clung to the king. But her struggles were of no avail . . .

Next day the mother found the place where the king was resting, surrounded by his attendants. She did not have to wait long. At the sight of this ugly old woman the king said, 'Old one, if you have a daughter, take note that I don't receive during the day.'

She looked him squarely in the eye. Her face was calm and impassive, and not a movement nor a gesture ruffled her bearing as she replied:

'Sire, by the look of you, anyone would think that you have no mother. From the day you were born until now, you have contended only with women, because they are weak. The pleasure you derive from it is more vile than the act itself. I'm not angry with you for behaving in that way. Because you are a man and because a woman is always a woman, and so Nature wills it. I'm not angry with you for you do have a mother, and through mothers I respect every human being. Son of a king or of a slave, the mother bears a child with love, gives birth in pain, and cherishes this rending of herself in the utmost depths of her senses. In her name I forgive you. Hold women in respect, not for their white hairs but for the sake of your own mother in the first place and then for womanhood itself. It is from woman that all greatness flows, whether of the ruler, of the warrior, the coward, the griot or musician ... In a mother's heart, the child is king ... All these people around you have a mother, and in their time of grief or of joy she sees but her child.'

'Kill her!' the king yelled.

But no one moved. The woman's words had gone home. The king roared and bellowed with anger, venting his spleen in a stream of vulgarities.

'You were all witnesses when he used your sisters,' the mother went on, without arrogance or pride. 'On his orders your fathers were put to death. And now he's putting his hands on your mothers and sisters. To look at you all, anyone would think you'd lost all sense of dignity.'

Beside himself with anger, the king suddenly stood up and gave the old mother a backhand blow that sent her reeling to the ground. He had no chance to do anything more, for he was seized and led away. For the first time, his subjects had been given the courage to revolt and put down their king.

Glory to all, men and women, who have had the courage to defy slanderous tongues. Praise to all women, unfailing well-springs of life, who are more powerful than death. Glory to you, coolies of Old China and the tagala-coye *of the Niger plateau! Glory to the wives of seamen in your everlasting mourning! Glory to thee, little child, little girl already playing at being the mother . . .*

The boundless ocean is as nothing beside the boundless tenderness of a mother.

7
Her Three Days

She raised her haggard face, and her far-away look ranged beyond the muddle of roofs, some tiled, others of thatch or galvanized-iron; the wide fronds of the twin coconut-palms were swaying slowly in the breeze, and in her mind she could hear their faint rustling. Noumbe was thinking of 'her three days'. Three days for her alone, when she would have her husband Mustapha to herself . . . It was a long time since she had felt such emotion. To have Mustapha! The thought comforted her. She had heart trouble and still felt some pain, but she had been dosing herself for the past two days, taking more medicine than was prescribed. It was a nice syrup that just slipped down, and she felt the beneficial effects at once. She blinked; her eyes were like two worn buttonholes, with lashes that were like frayed thread, in little clusters of fives and threes; the whites were the colour of old ivory.

'What's the matter, Noumbe?' asked Aida, her next-door neighbour, who was sitting at the door of her room.

'Nothing,' she answered, and went on cutting up the slice of raw meat, helped by her youngest daughter.

'Ah, it's your three days,' exclaimed Aida, whose words held a meaning that she could not elaborate on while the little girl was present. She went on: 'You're looking fine enough to prevent a holy man from saying his prayers properly!'

'Aida, be careful what you say,' she protested, a little annoyed.

But it was true; Noumbe had plaited her hair and put henna on her hands and feet. And that morning she had got the children up early to give her room a thorough clean. She was not old, but one pregnancy after another – and she had five children – and her heart trouble had aged her before her time.

'Go and ask Laity to give you five francs' worth of salt and twenty francs' worth of oil,' Noumbe said to the girl. 'Tell him I sent you. I'll pay for them as soon as your father is here, at midday.' She looked disapprovingly at the cut-up meat in the bottom of the bowl.

The child went off with the empty bottle and Noumbe got to her feet. She was thin and of average height. She went into her one-room shack, which was sparsely furnished; there was a bed with a white cover, and in one corner stood a table with pieces of china on display. The walls were covered with enlargements and photos of friends and strangers framed in passe-partout.

When she came out again she took the Moorish stove and set about lighting it.

Her daughter had returned from her errand.

'He gave them to you?' asked Noumbe.

'Yes, mother.'

A woman came across the compound to her. 'Noumbe, I can see that you're preparing a delicious dish.'

'Yes,' she replied. 'It's my three days. I want to revive the feasts of the old days, so that his palate will retain the taste of the dish for many moons, and he'll forget the cooking of his other wives.'

'Ah-ha! So that his palate is eager for dishes to come,' said the woman, who was having a good look at the ingredients.

'I'm feeling in good form,' said Noumbe, with some pride in her voice. She grasped the woman's hand and passed it over her loins.

'*Thieh, souya dome!* I hope you can say the same tomorrow morning . . .'

The woman clapped her hands; as if it were a signal or an invitation, other women came across, one with a metal jar, another with a saucepan, which they beat while the woman sang:

> *Sope dousa rafetaïl,*
> *Sopa nala dousa rafetail*

Sa yahi n'diguela.
(Worship of you is not for your beauty,
I worship you not for your beauty
But for your backbone.)

In a few moments, they improvised a wild dance to this chorus. At the end, panting and perspiring, they burst out laughing. Then one of them stepped into Noumbe's room and called the others.

'Let's take away the bed! Because tonight they'll wreck it!'

'She's right. Tomorrow this room will be . . .'

Each woman contributed an earthy comment which set them all laughing hilariously. Then they remembered they had work to do, and brought their amusement to an end; each went back to her family occupations.

Noumbe had joined in the laughter; she knew this boisterous 'ragging' was the custom in the compound. No one escaped it. Besides, she was an exceptional case, as they all knew. She had a heart condition and her husband had quite openly neglected her. Mustapha had not been to see her for a fortnight. All this time she had been hoping that he would come, if only for a moment. When she went to the clinic for mothers and children she compelled her youngest daughter to stay at home, so that – thus did her mind work – if her husband turned up the child could detain him until she returned. She ought to have gone to the clinic again this day, but she had spent what little money she possessed on preparing for Mustapha. She did not want her husband to esteem her less than his other wives, or to think her meaner. She did not neglect her duty as a mother, but her wifely duty came first – at certain times.

She imagined what the next three days would be like; already her 'three days' filled her whole horizon. She forgot her illness and her baby's ailments. She had thought about these three days in a thousand different ways. Mustapha would not leave before the Monday morning. In her mind she could see Mustapha and his henchmen crowding into her room, and could hear their suggestive jokes. 'If she had been a perfect wife . . .' She laughed to herself. 'Why shouldn't it always be like that for every woman – to have a husband of one's own?' She wondered why not.

The morning passed at its usual pace, the shadows of the coconut-palms and the people growing steadily shorter. As midday approached, the housewives busied themselves with the meal. In the compound each one stood near her door, ready to welcome her man. The kids were playing around, and their mothers' calls to them crossed in the air. Noumbe gave her children a quick meal and sent them out again. She sat waiting for Mustapha to arrive at any moment . . . he wouldn't be much longer now.

An hour passed, and the men began going back to work. Soon the compound was empty of the male element; the women, after a long siesta, joined one another under the coconut-palms and the sounds of their gossiping gradually increased.

Noumbe, weary of waiting, had finally given up keeping a lookout. Dressed in her mauve velvet, she had been on the watch since before midday. She had eaten no solid food, consoling herself with the thought that Mustapha would appear at any moment. Now she fought back the pangs of hunger by telling herself that in the past Mustapha had a habit of arriving late. In those days, this lateness was pleasant. Without admitting it to herself, those moments (which had hung terribly heavy) had been very sweet; they prolonged the sensual pleasure of anticipation. Although those minutes had been sometimes shot through with doubts and fears (often, very often, the thought of her coming disgrace had assailed her; for Mustapha, who had taken two wives before her, had just married another), they had not been too hard to bear. She realized that those demanding minutes were the price she had to pay for Mustapha's presence. Then she began to reckon up the score, in small ways, against the *veudieux*, the other wives. One washed his *boubous* when it was another wife's turn, or kept him long into the night; another sometimes held him in her embrace a whole day, knowing quite well that she was preventing Mustapha from carrying out his marital duty elsewhere.

She sulked as she waited; Mustapha had not been near her for a fortnight. All these bitter thoughts brought her up against reality: four months ago Mustapha had married a younger woman. This sudden realization of the facts sent a pain to her heart, a pain of anguish. The additional pain did not prevent her heart from functioning normally, rather was it like a sick person whose sleep banishes pain but who once awake again finds his suffering is as bad as ever, and pays for the relief by a redoubling of pain.

She took three spoonfuls of her medicine instead of the two prescribed, and felt a little better in herself.

She called her youngest daughter. 'Tell Mactar I want him.'

The girl ran off and soon returned with her eldest brother.

'Go and fetch your father,' Noumbe told him.

'Where, mother?'

'Where? Oh, on the main square or at one of your other mothers'.'

'But I've been to the main square already, and he wasn't there.'

'Well, go and have another look. Perhaps he's there now.'

The boy looked up at his mother, then dropped his head again and reluctantly turned to go.

'When your father has finished eating, I'll give you what's left. It's meat. Now be quick, Mactar.'

It was scorching hot and the clouds were riding high. Mactar was back after an hour. He had not found his father. Noumbe went and joined the group of women. They were chattering about this and that; one of them asked (just for the sake of asking), 'Noumbe, has your uncle (darling) arrived?' 'Not yet,' she replied, then hastened to add, 'Oh, he won't be long now. He knows it's my three days.' She deliberately changed the conversation in order to avoid a long discussion about the other three wives. But all the time she was longing to go and find Mustapha. She was being robbed of her three days. And the other wives knew it. Her hours alone with Mustapha were being snatched from her. The thought of his being with one of the other wives, who was feeding him and opening his waistcloth when she ought to be doing all that, who was enjoying those hours which were hers by right, so numbed Noumbe that it was impossible for her to react. The idea that

Mustapha might have been admitted to hospital or taken to a police station never entered her head.

She knew how to make tasty little dishes for Mustapha which cost him nothing. She never asked him for money. Indeed, hadn't she got herself into debt so that he would be more comfortable and have better meals at her place? And in the past, when Mustapha sometimes arrived unexpectedly – this was soon after he had married her – hadn't she hastened to make succulent dishes for him? All her friends knew this.

A comforting thought coursed through her and sent these aggressive and vindictive reflections to sleep. She told herself that Mustapha was bound to come to her this evening. The certainty of his presence stripped her mind of the too cruel thought that the time of her disfavour was approaching; this thought had been as much a burden to her as a heavy weight dragging a drowning man to the bottom. When all the bad, unfavourable thoughts besetting her had been dispersed, like piles of rubbish on waste land swept by a flood, the future seemed brighter, and she joined in the conversation of the women with childish enthusiasm, unable to hide her pleasure and her hopes. It was like something in a parcel; questioning eyes wondered what was inside, but she alone knew and enjoyed the secret, drawing an agreeable strength from it. She took an active part in the talking and brought her wit into play. All this vivacity sprang from the joyful conviction that Mustapha would arrive this evening very hungry and be hers alone.

In the far distance, high above the tree-tops, a long trail of dark-grey clouds tinged with red was hiding the sun. The time for the *tacousane*, the afternoon prayer, was drawing near. One by one, the women withdrew to their rooms, and the shadows of the trees grew longer, wider and darker.

Night fell; a dark, starry night.

Noumbe cooked some rice for the children. They clamoured in vain for some of the meat. Noumbe was stern and unyielding: 'The meat is for your father. He didn't eat at midday.' When she had fed the children, she washed herself again to get rid of the smell of cooking and touched up her toilette, rubbing oil on her hands, feet and legs to make the henna more brilliant. She intended to remain by her door, and sat down on the bench; the incense smelt strongly, filling the whole room. She was facing the entrance to the compound and could see the other women's husbands coming in.

But for her there was no one.

She began to feel tired again. Her heart was troubling her, and she had a fit of coughing. Her inside seemed to be on fire. Knowing that she would not be going to the dispensary during her 'three days', in order to economize, she went and got some wood-ash which she mixed with water and drank. It did not taste very nice, but it would make the medicine last longer, and the drink checked and soothed the burning within her for a while. She was tormenting herself with the thoughts passing through her mind. Where can he be? With the first wife? No, she's quite old. The second then? Everyone knew that she was out of favour with Mustapha. The third wife was herself. So he must be with the fourth. There were puckers of uncertainty and doubt in the answers she gave herself. She kept putting back the time to go to bed, like a lover who does not give up waiting when the time of the rendezvous is long past, but with an absurd and stupid hope waits still longer, self-torture and the heavy minutes chaining him to the spot. At each step Noumbe took, she stopped and mentally explored the town, prying into each house inhabited by one of the other wives. Eventually she went indoors.

So that she would not be caught unawares by Mustapha nor lose the advantages which her make-up and good clothes gave her, she lay down on the bed fully dressed and alert. She had turned down the lamp as far as possible, so the room was dimly lit. But she fell asleep despite exerting great strength of mind to remain awake and saying repeatedly to herself, 'I shall wait for him.' To make sure that she would be standing there expectantly when he crossed the threshold, she had bolted the door. Thus she would be the devoted wife, always ready to serve her husband, having got up at once and appearing as elegant as if it were broad daylight. She had even thought of making a gesture as she stood there, of passing her hands casually over her hips so that Mustapha would hear the clinking of the beads she had strung round her waist and be incited to look at her from head to foot.

Morning came, but there was no Mustapha.

When the children awoke they asked if their father had come. The oldest of them, Mactar, a promising lad, was quick to spot that his mother had not made the bed, that the bowl containing the stew was still in the same place, by a dish of rice, and the loaf of bread on the table was untouched. The children got a taste of their mother's anger. The youngest, Amadou, took a long time over dressing. Noumbe hurried them up and sent the youngest girl to Laity's to buy five francs' worth of ground coffee. The children's breakfast was warmed-up rice with a meagre sprinkling of gravy from the previous day's stew. Then she gave them their wings, as the saying goes, letting them all out except the youngest daughter. Noumbe inspected the bottle of medicine and saw that she had taken a lot of it; there were only three spoonfuls left. She gave herself half a spoonful and made up for the rest with her mixture of ashes and water. After that she felt calmer.

'Why, Noumbe, you must have got up bright and early this morning, to be so dressed up. Are you going off on a long journey?'

It was Aida, her next-door neighbour, who was surprised to see her dressed in such a manner, especially for a woman who was having 'her three days'. Then Aida realized what had happened and tried to rectify her mistake.

'Oh, I see he hasn't come yet. They're all the same, these men!'

'He'll be here this morning, Aida.' Noumbe bridled, ready to defend her man. But it was rather her own worth she was defending, wanting to conceal what an awful time she had spent. It had been a broken night's sleep, listening to harmless sounds which she had taken for Mustapha's footsteps, and this had left its mark on her already haggard face.

'I'm sure he will! I'm sure he will!' exclaimed Aida, well aware of this comedy that all the women played in turn.

'Mustapha is such a kind man, and so noble in his attitude,' added another woman, rubbing it in.

'If he weren't, he wouldn't be my master,' said Noumbe, feeling flattered by this description of Mustapha.

The news soon spread round the compound that Mustapha had slept elsewhere during Noumbe's three days. The other women pitied her. It was against all the rules for Mustapha to spend a night elsewhere. Polygamy had its laws, which should be respected. A sense of decency and common dignity restrained a wife from keeping the husband day and night when his whole person and everything connected with him belonged to another wife during 'her three days'. The game, however, was not without its underhand tricks that one wife played on another; for instance, to wear out the man and hand him over when he was incapable of performing his conjugal duties. When women criticized the practice of polygamy they always found that the wives were to blame, especially those who openly dared to play a dirty trick. The man was whitewashed. He was a weakling who always ended by falling into the enticing traps set for him by woman. Satisfied with this conclusion, Noumbe's neighbours made common cause with her and turned to abusing Mustapha's fourth wife.

Noumbe made some coffee – she never had any herself, because of her heart. She consoled herself with the thought that Mustapha would find more things at her place. The bread had gone stale; she would buy some more when he arrived.

The hours dragged by again, long hours of waiting which became harder to bear as the day progressed. She wished she knew where he was . . . The thought obsessed her, and her eyes became glazed and searching. Every time she heard a man's voice she straightened up quickly. Her heart was paining her more and more, but the physical pain was separate from the mental one; they never came together, alternating in a way that reminded her of the acrobatic feat of a man riding two speeding horses.

At about four o'clock Noumbe was surprised to see Mustapha's second wife appear at the door. She had come to see if Mustapha was there, knowing that it was Noumbe's three days. She did not tell Noumbe the reason for her wishing to see Mustapha, despite being pressed. So Noumbe concluded that it was largely due to jealousy, and was pleased that the other wife could see how clean and tidy her room was, and what a display of fine things she had, all of which could hardly fail to make the other think that Mustapha had been (and still was) very generous to her, Noumbe. During the rambling conversation her heart thumped ominously, but she bore up and held off taking any medicine.

Noumbe remembered only too well that when she was newly married she had usurped the second wife's three days. At that time she had been the youngest wife. Mustapha had not let a day pass without coming to see her. Although not completely certain, she believed she had conceived her third child during this wife's three days. The latter's presence now and remarks that she let drop made Noumbe realize that she was no longer the favourite. This revelation, and the polite, amiable tone and her visitor's eagerness to inquire after her children's health and her own, to praise her superior choice of household utensils, her taste in clothes, the cleanliness of the room and the lingering fragrance of the incense, all this was like a stab in cold blood, a cruel reminder of the perfidy of words and the hypocrisy of rivals; and all part of the world of women. This observation did not get her anywhere, except to arouse a desire to escape from the circle of polygamy and to cause her to ask herself – it was a moment of mental aberration really – 'Why do we allow ourselves to be men's playthings?'

The other wife complimented her and insisted that Noumbe's children should go and spend a few days with her own children (in this she was sincere). By accepting in principle, Noumbe was weaving her own waist-cloth of hypocrisy. It was all to make the most of herself, to set tongues wagging so that she would lose none of her respectability and rank. The other wife casually added – before she forgot, as she said – that she wanted to see Mustapha, and if mischief-makers told Noumbe that 'their' husband had been to see her during Noumbe's three days, Noumbe shouldn't think ill of her, and she would rather have seen him here to tell him what she had to say. To save face, Noumbe dared not ask her when she had last seen Mustapha. The other would have replied with a smile, 'The last morning of my three days, of course. I've only come here because it's urgent.' And Noumbe would have looked embarrassed and put on an air of innocence. 'No, that isn't what I meant. I just wondered if you had happened to meet him by chance.'

Neither of them would have lost face. It was all that remained to them. They were not lying, to their way of thinking. Each had been desired and spoilt for a time; then the man, like a gorged vulture, had left them on one side and the venom of chagrin at having been mere playthings had entered their hearts. They quite understood, it was all quite clear to them, that they could sink no lower; so they clung to what was left to them, that is to say, to saving what dignity remained to them by false words and gaining advantages at the expense of the other. They did not indulge in this game for the sake of it. This falseness contained all that remained of the flame of dignity. No one was taken in, certainly not themselves. Each knew that the other was lying, but neither could bring herself to further humiliation, for it would be the final crushing blow.

The other wife left. Noumbe almost propelled her to the door, then stood there thoughtful for a few moments. Noumbe understood the reason for the other's visit. She had come to get her own back. Noumbe felt absolutely sure that Mustapha was with his latest wife. The visit meant in fact: 'You stole those days from me because I am older than you. Now a younger woman than you is avenging me. Try as you might to make everything nice and pleasant for him, you have to toe the line with the rest of us now, you old carcass. He's slept with someone else – and he will again.'

The second day passed like the first, but was more dreadful. She ate no proper food, just enough to stave off the pangs of hunger.

It was Sunday morning and all the men were at home; they nosed about in one room and another, some of them cradling their youngest in their arms, others playing with the older children. The draught-players had gathered in one place, the card-players in another. There was a friendly atmosphere in the compound, with bursts of happy laughter and sounds of guttural voices, while the women busied themselves with the housework.

Aida went to see Noumbe to console her, and said without much conviction, 'He'll probably come today. Men always seem to have something to do at the last minute. It's Sunday today, so he'll be here.'

'Aida, Mustapha doesn't work,' Noumbe pointed out, hard-eyed. She gave a cough. 'I've been waiting for him now for two days and nights! When it's my three days I think the least he could do is to be here – at night, anyway. I might die . . .'

'Do you want me to go and look for him?'

'No.'

She had thought 'yes'. It was the way in which Aida had made the offer that embarrassed her. Of course she would like her to! Last night, when everyone had gone to bed, she had started out and covered quite some distance before turning back. The flame of her dignity had been fanned on the way. She did not want to abase herself still further by going to claim a man who seemed to have no desire to see her. She had lain awake until dawn, thinking it all over and telling herself that her marriage to Mustapha was at an end, that she would divorce him. But this morning there was a tiny flicker of hope in her heart: 'Mustapha will come, all the same. This is my last night.'

She borrowed a thousand francs from Aida, who readily lent her the money. And she followed the advice to send the children off again, to Mustapha's fourth wife.

'Tell him that I must see him at once, I'm not well!'

She hurried off to the little market near by and bought a chicken and several other things. Her eyes were feverishly, joyfully bright as she carefully added seasoning to the dish she prepared. The appetizing smell of her cooking was wafted out to the compound and its Sunday atmosphere. She swept the room again, shut the door and windows, but the heady scent of the incense escaped through the cracks between the planks.

The children returned from their errand.

'Is he ill?' she asked them.

'No, mother. He's going to come. We found him with some of his friends at Voulimata's (the fourth wife). He asked about you.'

'And that's all he said?'

'Yes, mother.'

'Don't come indoors. Here's ten francs. Go and play somewhere else.'

A delicious warm feeling spread over her. 'He was going to come.' Ever since Friday she had been harbouring spiteful words to throw in his face. He would beat her, of course . . . But never mind. Now she found it would be useless to utter those words. Instead she would do everything possible to make up for the lost days. She was happy, much too happy to bear a grudge against him, now that she knew he was coming – he might even be on the way with his henchmen. The only means of getting her own back was to cook a big meal . . . then he would stay in bed.

She finished preparing the meal, had a bath and went on to the rest of her toilette. She did her hair again, put antimony on her lower lip, eyebrows and lashes, then dressed in a white starched blouse and a hand-woven waist-cloth, and inspected her hands and feet. She was quite satisfied with her appearance.

But the waiting became prolonged.

No one in the compound spoke to her for fear of hurting her feelings. She had sat down outside the door, facing the entrance to the compound, and the other inhabitants avoided meeting her sorrowful gaze. Her tears overflowed the brim of her eyes like a swollen river its banks; she tried to hold them back, but in vain. She was eating her heart out.

The sound of a distant tom-tom was being carried on the wind. Time passed over her, like the seasons over monuments. Twilight came and darkness fell.

On the table were three plates in a row, one for each day.

'I've come to keep you company,' declared Aida as she entered the room. Noumbe was sitting on the foot of the bed – she had fled from the silence of the others. 'You mustn't get worked up about it,' went on Aida. 'Every woman goes through it. Of course it's not nice! But I don't think he'll be long now.'

Noumbe raised a moist face and bit her lips nervously. Aida saw that she had made up her mind not to say anything.

Everything was shrouded in darkness; no light came from her room. After supper, the children had refrained from playing their noisy games.

Just when adults were beginning to feel sleepy and going to bed, into the compound walked Mustapha, escorted by two of his lieutenants. He was clad entirely in white. He greeted the people still about in an oily manner, then invited his companions into Noumbe's hut.

She had not stirred.

'Wife, where's the lamp?'

'Where you left it this morning when you went out.'

'How are you?' inquired Mustapha when he had lit the lamp. He went and sat down on the bed, and motioned to the two men to take the bench.

'God be praised,' Noumbe replied to his polite inquiry. Her thin face seemed relaxed and the angry lines had disappeared.

'And the children?'

'They're well, praise be to God.'

'Our wife isn't very talkative this evening,' put in one of the men.

'I'm quite well, though.'

'Your heart isn't playing you up now?' asked Mustapha, not unkindly.

'No, it's quite steady,' she answered.

'God be praised! Mustapha, we'll be off,' said the man, uncomfortable at Noumbe's cold manner.

'Wait,' said Mustapha, and turned to Noumbe. 'Wife, are we eating tonight or tomorrow?'

'Did you leave me something when you went out this morning?'

'What? That's not the way to answer.'

'No, uncle (darling). I'm just asking . . . Isn't it right?'

Mustapha realized that Noumbe was mocking him and trying to humiliate him in front of his men.

'You do like your little joke. Don't you know it's your three days?'

'Oh, uncle, I'm sorry, I'd quite forgotten. What an unworthy wife I am!' she exclaimed, looking straight at Mustapha.

'You're making fun of me!'

'Oh, uncle, I shouldn't dare! What, I? And who would help me into Paradise, if not my worthy husband? Oh, I would never poke fun at you, neither in this world nor the next.'

'Anyone would think so.'

'Who?' she asked.

'You might have stood up when I came in, to begin with . . .'

'Oh, uncle, forgive me. I'm out of my mind with joy at seeing you again. But whose fault is that, uncle?'

'And just what are these three plates for?' said Mustapha with annoyance.

'These three plates?' She looked at him, a malicious smile on her lips. 'Nothing. Or rather, my three days. Nothing that would interest you. Is there anything here that interests you . . . uncle?'

As if moved by a common impulse, the three men stood up.

Noumbe deliberately knocked over one of the plates. 'Oh, uncle, forgive me . . .' Then she broke the other two plates. Her eyes had gone red; suddenly a pain stabbed at her heart, she bent double, and as she fell to the floor gave a loud groan which roused the whole compound.

Some women came hurrying in. 'What's the matter with her?'

'Nothing . . . only her heart. Look what she's done, the silly woman. One of these days her jealousy will suffocate her. I haven't been to see her – only two days, and she cries her eyes out. Give her some ash and she'll be all right,' gabbled Mustapha, and went off.

'Now these hussies have got their associations, they think they're going to run the country,' said one of his men.

'Have you heard that at Bamako they passed a resolution condemning polygamy?' added the other. 'Heaven preserve us from having only one wife.'

'They can go out to work then,' pronounced Mustapha as he left the compound.

Aida and some of the women lifted Noumbe on to the bed. She was groaning. They got her to take some of her mixture of ash and water . . .

8
Letters from France

Marseilles

My dear old friend,

You're sulking. You're sulking without knowing anything about
my state of mind and my material circumstances here. To be sure,
if I did as you say, I ought to have written to you more often.
Haven't you received my letters? (Oh! don't stick your bottom lip
out – I know you still do that.) If my letters are too short it's because
I couldn't do otherwise. Believe me. I need you to believe me.

You know you're the only one I love and want for my friend.
Stop sulking! I admit I've been in the wrong. Hurry and send me
your news, the news of everyone.

As to my husband, I'll tell you about him later. You'll have a
shock, my girl. Poor stupid fool that I was.

Your old and frank friend,
Nafi.

Marseilles

Dear old friend,

I've read your letter at least twenty times, my father's letter just
the once. Father had written to my husband – I emphasize the word
'husband' as it contains something quite different from what a girl
usually expects of the man she marries. Well, my 'husband' said to
me, there's a letter from your father. After he'd had it read to him
by someone else. For he can't read, my old man. And he is old, is
my husband. That's not so serious as the rest. The rest is a lot
worse!

Don't forget to write. Write even if you don't get anything from me. Hoping to hear from you, I send you fond kisses.

Yours ever, Nafi.

Dear old friend,

I can't reply to all your questions. A flood of questions! I don't know where to begin myself. For days I've been looking out for the postman, morning and afternoon. I was afraid of my 'husband' intercepting my letters. I think he's quite capable of that. But he goes out in the afternoons. Not in the mornings though. Just after he'd gone out, I saw Mister Postman come. Your letter was there. The woman who manages this block of furnished rooms gave me an odd look, as if to say, 'Your daddy of a husband has given orders not to hand over the mail to anyone.' But I didn't let her get away with it. Nevertheless, I'm obliged to tell Monsieur that there was a letter for me.

No, I haven't got persecution mania. You know me very well. Let me tell you, my dear old friend, all the joys that your letters bring me – an intoxication of sunshine, heat that makes my body exude torrents, waves of pulsations which send the warm blood edged with foam that's laced with bracing memories surging through my whole being (inside and out). I've never realized that memories are so necessary.

I haven't any sun here. I live shut up between the four walls of a block of furnished rooms that's shabby and dirty, damp, smelly, and without running water or proper toilets. I'm so much alone that sometimes I talk to myself aloud. A prisoner of the thick shadows of dreary walls oozing in summer and winter alike, that's what I am. When my gaze happens to wander it meets with nothing but cracks encrusted with ancient grey dust or a bare tiled floor all scored and scratched. Most of the time, I'm indoors. Where could I go? Who with? Him? No. There's one room for both of us. A room that has to do for cooking and washing. If I want to do a job for myself during the night, I don't go out; I use the chamber-pot. There's one lavatory and one tap for all the tenants. My room – no, that's a pretension – my 'husband's' room is what is called a 'dark room'. It's right opposite the stairs, so the door has to be kept shut all the time, as is the rule in this country. Above the only door there's a small opening, but the sun never gets round to it. To do my work, I have the light on all the time. How could all this not be bound to affect me, to influence my character?

Do you remember how lively I was, overflowing with vitality? Everyone used to talk of my exuberance. Well, now I'm all shrivelled up, like a slice of meat left in the sun. To be sure, I used to live in a hovel in a shanty-town. But there was an abundance of sunshine and much laughter; there were shared pleasures and hopes. Here there's nothing. Nothing, I tell you. Sometimes in my thoughts I can see the lesions hollowed out by the bloody weepings of my heart. And then I ask questions.

To see the sun I have to go out and walk to the nearest cross-roads. And then, in a gap between the buildings and on the stroke of two, the orb deigns to show itself – though not every day, it depends. Here the sun has no strength, it's timid and doesn't blaze down very much. And the women hang out their washing from the day before. How sad it all is.

My dear, you can't possibly imagine my disillusionment. When you and the others are chatting together I expect you say that Nafi is in France – and everyone envies me! But I'm not in France, at least not the France that came into our dreams and fed our ambitions. I'm in a different world, a gloomy, depressing world which weighs me down, is slowly killing me off, day by day.

A photo has made an outcast of me.

How I regret ever marrying . . . It's my own fault, I know. I am the victim of a mirage. My father showed me a photo of a man; he looked handsome, and he was in France. A few days later my father said to me: 'This man wants you for his wife. He is in France, he works there. He's been living there for years.' That was all. For weeks, I put off giving my answer. Then I accepted him, although there were many young men of my age who wanted me. Granted, with any of them, I'd never have visited France. And what school-

girl has not dreamed of France, of Paris and the brightly-lit avenues?
So I consented. Why? For France. For her, the artificial France, I
gave up all my suitors. Now I've got what I deserved – doubly so.
Really, I never thought I should sink so low. I'm ashamed to tell
the whole story. How I should like to see our sunshine again, the
garish colours, and the nonchalance of our women sauntering to
market in joyful groups; to hear again the arguments going on
around the public fountain, to chaff the men selling shins of beef, to
catch the sounds of a kora through the hubbub of the daily round,
to sit in the shade out of the blinding sun, to see the chickens standing on one leg, and children going on errands wearing their father's
sandals, hugging the fence.

I'm lonely, so lonely that I envy the corpses in their graves. I've
no taste for anything. Everything has lost its flavour. The food here
always needs to be seasoned. But my 'husband' can't stand the taste
of red peppers, his old stomach won't take them any more. If, in
compensation, there were enough sun I might get used to him, in
spite of his age. I've had enough, I've touched bottom.

I'll tell you about him . . . Where shall I begin? The day I arrived?
That morning – six months ago, that was. Don't tell me time passes
quickly. Half a year in hell would have been sweeter. You remember
the photo I gave to Aminata? Well, that's him. A photo taken
twenty years ago! And like a perfect idiot, I was taken in by it. By a
photo that had been touched up! He's seventy-three. It says so on
his sworn affidavit. He doesn't know the exact date of his birth.
But he looks younger. A cold climate preserves Africans. For the
rest, he's as hale and hearty as any man . . . the swine! In spite of all
my pleas, I have to go through with it. His eyes have lost their
brightness, they're just dull and lifeless.

His job is being out of work. That's lasted five years. Every
afternoon he makes the rounds of the shipping companies' offices.
He sells kola-nuts – wholesale or retail. He never goes out without
his jar filled with nuts. The other day he said to me, 'The whites are
beginning to realize the benefits of kola-nuts.' He walks slowly. I
get the impression that he walks sideways, although I've never yet

c

seen him coming towards me from more than five yards away. He goes out by himself, comes back by himself, the jar empty – or half empty. After he's said the evening prayer he counts his takings. I see his bent back as he reckons his day's earnings, then he puts it all in an old school satchel which he keeps always in the same place. Sometimes old men of his age come and visit him, and they all natter away about things my generation knows nothing of. They talk over their past. I go to bed, keeping my ears cocked to their nostalgic reminiscences of their youth. All about the failure of a certain policy, a certain world – the elders who accepted the domination of the foreigner through their passive resistance. About this almost total submission which was fed by the promise of an everlasting ease in the future. It all makes me feel very bitter, and rightly so.

My dear old friend, I don't rebel against my situation. Do you remember what we used to dream about – of what life would bring us, of the house we should like to live in and how it would be with our husband and our children? Do you remember, too, how we used to carry on so angrily against polygamy?

When I look back and remember my childhood, the big house filled with the cries of children, with singing and sunshine, my loneliness terrifies me. There are times when I wish I could catch some awful disease, an illness with running sores, so that my appearance would put him off and he would not want to touch me. I suffer from not being ill . . .

Well, that's enough for you to envy me for. As you say you envy me, make quite sure my letter doesn't get into other hands, especially my parents'. I embrace you. If you see Tave, give him my good wishes but don't say a word about my troubles.

Fond kisses from Nafi.

My dear,

No news is good news! Yes, but I need news. Your news, warm with our sun and sprinkled with the gossip around the fountain, the trifling kind as well as the other.

My 'husband' has just gone out, so I'm taking advantage to continue our conversation of a month or so ago. I have to go and see Madame Baronne. She's a very nice woman who has a grocery shop down the street. I keep her company, or rather the opposite is nearer the truth. I got your letter yesterday.

I'm alone with you, just as when there were only the two of us. With you, I can pour my heart out. You're a real friend, something truly rare. You say you're surprised by what I told you about the great age of my 'husband'? If I went further into details of his state, you'd be flabbergasted. By your suppositions, you raise doubts in my mind. It's quite true, and I've thought about it myself, that my marriage to Demba was hatched in silence to which my father contributed. It's a thought that sometimes gnaws sharply at my mind. Yet I refuse to believe it. Not for myself, but for a reason I'm unable to determine for the moment. What I can be certain of, if these doubts should prove to have substance, is that the little shame remaining to me would be still further diluted. I find consolation in the fact that I brought my misfortunes on myself. But to know that I was caught in a plot which was chiefly the work of my father, my own father . . . no, that I can't believe. You know my father, how gentle, good and straightforward he is.

Why do you go on hurting me? No, my friend, I believe you're sincere. It's just that to know such things is very unpleasant.

You don't believe me? It's unpleasant all the same! I assure you that he's as old as my father, if not older. Besides, I'm enclosing one of his papers. His body is all creased. Now that winter is upon us – and it's devilishly cold, I'm all curdled – he wears long underpants night and day. He washes in the room. In the evening – the hardest moment of all for me is when he comes to bed. That's all he thinks of. Anyone would believe he's after getting an heir. I detest him to the point of hating my own body. His death would be a happy release for me. Sometimes, to break the silence, he tells me about episodes in his past, the pig. He's been up to plenty of mischief, if I'm to believe all he says. Our talk is at cross-purposes.

But I can say it to you. I think I'm going to have a baby. And the other evening, after gazing at me a long time – the swine – he said, 'You ought to go and see a doctor.' It was he who first pointed out my condition. After all, he ought to know all about the subject, considering the time he's been gallivanting about the ports. And he added, without giving me time to recover, 'If the doctor gives you a certificate to say that you're pregnant, we'll go to the shipping company and you can see the chief in charge of sailings.' He's the one who engages the crews. For five years now, my 'husband' has been out of work. 'The white women do that for their husbands,' he ended up. 'Why shouldn't we do the same?'

If you knew how humiliating it was to hear him say that to me! It wasn't enough to send me off my nut, he expected me to go and make eyes at some white or other, too.

I can hear his voice through the skylight. He's coming back; I'll leave you until later.

I'm taking up our chat again. As I was saying, I went and saw the doctor. There's no doubt about it! I'm expecting. He's pleased, and he's always hanging around. He's more often in the room, with his foul smell, than out in the street. His mere presence fills me with disgust, more and more so. All his kindness and fond attentions just irritate me. He even goes and does some of my shopping for me, very likely because he's afraid I might get knocked down by a car while crossing the road. If only that could happen to me! What luck! But no, it's too much to hope for. So much the worse for me.

Just imagine, yesterday I went to see this shipping boss. Humiliating it was. This gentleman gave me an interview. He thought I was Demba's daughter. When I'd explained the object of my visit, assuming the air of a wife whose husband has been out of work for years and who is expecting her first baby, has no money and no hope of any to buy the layette – I probably sounded the right note there – this gentleman sent for the file on Demba and then said, 'Your husband has reached the age limit' (and he gazed at me with his globular eyes as if to say 'he could be your grandfather'), 'and with these modern techniques it will be difficult to find him a ship,

especially as a stoker. For we haven't any coal-burning vessels now.
And the modern ones . . .'

When it comes to being modern, my 'husband' is that all right.
A tight jacket and wide floppy trousers. He was waiting for me
down below, and before I left him to go up he had said, 'Insist on a
cleaner's job for me, as I don't know anything about the workings
of things on board.' So with that in mind, I pressed for a job for
him as a cleaner. And I pushed his claim with persistence, saying
that he'd been with the shipping company for more than thirty
years, and that now he was getting on in years they wanted nothing
more to do with him. He hadn't been given a pension, not even a
sum of money as compensation. Then I enlarged upon my situation
as an expectant mother, the rent, the high cost of living – everything
I could think of. I must have been more than half-an-hour in that
office. In the end, he gave way, he'll sign him on the first chance he
gets, 'and it'll be his last ship'.

So now you know and can see how I've spent the last couple of
days.

By that evening the news of my visit to the shipping office had
got around. After supper, his friends and acquaintances arrived one
after the other, all of his generation. They stank of tobacco and
never stopped chewing kola-nuts. I think Demba must have told
them that I'm expecting a baby, for they showed great concern
towards me. I looked at them as I listened to their talk, not saying a
word myself. They would suddenly fall silent, as if wanting to
retain in their hearing the last sentence someone had uttered. Now
and again they would stay quite still, body and jaws motionless –
like kids made to stand in the corner. Seeing them stuck like that,
not moving, made me think of those war-memorials with a statue
that no one puts flowers on except once a year. Their eyes have an
aged look, dulled by an infinite sadness, a sense of being neglected,
of living in a little world of their own, and only light up with their
last look to the past.

All they can do is re-open the past, their past. They talk about
the early years of this century, about the First World War, as I talk

to you about the present and dream of a better future. They recall the names of ships that were sunk, their tonnage, their captains and boatswains, the good and bad whites – for to them there still exist good and bad whites – and they recall old comrades now dead. And when one of them brings the conversation round to his childhood, they listen so religiously that I have the feeling he's making his confession, with his voice heavy with regrets. By dint of telling the same things over and over again, each one knows the other as if he were a part of himself. In the matter of growing up, they have many memories in common. Their characters were formed in the same way and their mentality is all alike.

These recollections help and support them, give them a link with their childhood . . . It's all they have left – a tarnished mirror giving a reflection of their youth. The life of an exile! They are doubly exiled – cut off from their origins and from the French language. And the present time, with its many changes, geographical, technical and mental, is quite beyond their comprehension. It is too late for them to return to their own country; they would be just as much foreigners there . . . They keep alive the events of the past and chew them over, make a meal of them in the present.

You can detect nostalgia in the tone of their voices, but they never seem disgruntled – indifferent is more the word. And there they are stuck here, stoically waiting for death to cart them off one after the other. And as their numbers decrease, so the remainder cling together more than ever.

It's an odd sort of life that these men lead.

You write and say that Tave has got married to that hussy! However did she manage to hook him? Tave is sensible and level-headed after all! She was only interested in ministers, deputies and heads of departments. Is it known who the father of her child is? Poor Tave! He's become a saver of dignity, a redeemer of sins. I've sometimes thought of writing to him, in moments of great loneliness and when smitten with remorse. He was the kindest and most sincere of all my suitors. I think it was his great kindness that curbed my desire for him. And now he's with this woman whom I never want to see. Let's hope that they'll be happy together until the divorce.

I'm very glad about you, from all you tell me. Of all us girls, you're the only one who has kept her head.

What a long letter! I shan't read it over, there's too much of it.

Yours ever,
Nafi.

Dear old friend,

Why this tone? This scarcely concealed wrath? For nearly two months you've been very cool with me. It's impossible for you to put yourself in my place. Besides, I shouldn't advise you to . . . No, I don't spend my time bemoaning my lot. I'm not living – I leave life on one side. It's worse! No one but me knows my mental sufferings.

Get a divorce? I don't think so. I'm too far from home to indulge in such a luxury. But thank you for your advice. I know, my marriage is a Muslim one. It's not valid in the eyes of the law. But which law? The law made by men or by the morals of men? I can leave him – that's true! But then where can I go? Who will take me in? Don't forget that I've no money to pay for my passage back to Dakar. Of course it's easy to bring about a break. And the baby – have you thought of that? No, I think you're on the wrong track. And I don't consider myself to be the centre of the universe either. At least, not now.

I've had a letter from my family, from my brother Babacar. I had a job to read it, so badly is it written. He asks me to get him a suit. Me – who never have any money! Where could I get any from? I've nothing of my own, absolutely nothing. My father has written to my 'husband', who is sending him some things. When I think . . . or rather when suspicion distils its poison in my heart, I'm deeply hurt. All filial love takes flight.

Do you remember our dreams, our ambitions when we were girls? We wanted to be free of a husband's domination, to be our own mistresses, be able to buy what we wished without having to give reasons for it or to wait for someone else to hand over the money to pay for it – in short, to be independent. Well, I haven't a chance now. With my old man's jar of kola-nuts and his being out of work, we just manage to live. Everything is very dear in France. The white men and women I know here all want to go to Africa. Sometimes my old man brings in packets of spaghetti and sugar, and where do you think he gets them from? The Welfare Committee. The tickets fell from his pocket one day. I found out about it by asking Madame Baronne. So you see what I've come to, begging. I tell myself I've got no morals left. Besides, Madame Baronne often tells me there are two kinds of morals, one for the rich and the other for the workers. And after thinking deeply about it, I came to the conclusion that she's quite right. Another thing – all hope of returning home hangs on playing the horses. My 'husband' has a bet on the Tote forecast every Sunday. He studies the racing page of the paper on Saturdays; crouched in a corner, he juggles with the names of horses. You ought to see him! He talks in millions, and on Sunday evening grumbles because one horse has let him down.

Poor wretch! It's the only hope left to him.

To reassure you of all my friendship for you, I'm keeping this letter short. My pregnancy is developing normally. I haven't yet written to tell my family. So don't you say anything to anybody. One never knows!

Many kisses, Nafi.

My very dear,

Something wonderful! There's a break in even the deepest gloom at times. Oh yes! I've just emerged from my long slumber of loneliness and despair, from my lethargy. I've left the bed I've been tied to for months – a bed of resignation. It's a little as if my whole horizon has been set alight.

My old man, my 'husband', joined his ship and sailed today. But wait! That's not the reason why I'm feeling so satisfied.

Where shall I begin? With the old man? The swine. If you knew how he takes everyone in, me included. He was sent a form to go and have a medical examination. He got someone else to go in his place. The doctor didn't notice anything – only black. In that way, his great age won't affect the doctor's opinion.

As the day of his departure drew near, so my life of isolation seemed to deepen. I was going to be really alone. I asked him to send me back to Africa, and I'd wait for him there. These dark, damp, cold walls seemed to be my coffin. I began to regret him – to say the opposite would be lying to you. He's my companion, the only person I could break the wall of silence with; as you know, I don't like him, but I was used to him. In this life of a recluse, he was all I had; and I'd got used to him a bit, as one gets used to some infirmity. He brought me news of the outside world. The long hours I spent with him – the time he took over his prayers, counting his money, his daily takings – that all filled the emptiness around me. And all that was going to be just a memory. We chatted together; we laughed. At the end I think I came to cherish his white hairs.

You remember the fable of the hyena? He won the most beautiful female in a competition open to all the animals, and his beaten rivals said to him, 'Hyena, you're much too ugly for her.' And he replied: 'I know. I know I'm not pleasant to look at. But that's because of all of you. When she sees no one but me for weeks and months on end, she'll start to get used to the sight of me and finish by liking me.' And the hyena was right.

He's made me a monthly allowance from his wages.

He joined a 'libert' ship – I'm not sure of the spelling and I haven't got a dictionary, but it's something like that.

And that's when it all started.

I went down to the docks with him, and he took me on board and proudly introduced me to his shipmates. I got the feeling that they were only looking at my belly and his wrinkled face, and were making rude jokes about his age. I was thinking about myself all the time – lonesome Nafi, my mind ran. While sitting down below in a cabin and ruminating on the future, I heard a loud voice say,

'Sister, it's time to leave.' It was him. Tall, thin. He wasn't even looking at me. He has a grave, pugnacious face, nothing sleek about it. He was wearing a blue suit – it's called Shanghai blue, I don't know why. 'Arona will take you back,' said my 'husband', poking his worn old face round the door. Their two faces filled my whole vision. 'If you need to know anything, Arona will help you,' added my 'husband'. He gave me some last advice and then accompanied me to the gangway. Arona was talking with some of the crew, a cigarette between his lips.

Then we walked out of the docks together, not saying a word. A white – who probably knew Arona – said to him, 'Is that your wife?' 'No, she's the wife of an old man,' he replied. I didn't know where to put myself. Wasn't his reply a dividing line? He was already keeping his distance. If you'd seen how he twice repeated 'No, no' – it was quite explicit. The white shook my hand all the same.

We took a bus to the Old Port, and during the journey got to know each other better. He had been on board the day I arrived here. And I knew him by name too – the old ones often talked about him. He pulled a face when I told him that. I know he's one of the leaders of the Association of Black Workers in France – a militant, in short.

When we got off the bus he helped me to cross the road, holding me by the elbow. Submissively, I allowed myself to be led. Out on the square there was an African sun, and in my heart too, shedding a flood of light. There were crowds of people walking about and long lines of cars moving slowly past. He took me to a café, a select one facing the port, and we had a drink.

How long we stayed there chatting away, I've no idea. What does it matter! All I know is, it was wonderful! And besides, I was in no hurry to get back to my attic room with its tatty walls, thick shadows and damp sheets, where I should be all alone. The din all around was deafening – the hooting of cars, a pneumatic drill where workmen were mending the road, and the cacophony of the crowds.

I was feeling fine in heart and body. This sequel to the gloomy, silent days made my face radiant, and a flood of joyfulness surged through my veins. The hyena was right: 'I know that, I know I'm not pleasant to look at. And it's because of all of you. But when she sees no one but me, me alone, for weeks and months on end, she'll start to get used to the sight of me and finish by liking me.'

Arona was not looking at me; in fact we hardly caught each other's glance. He was sitting at his ease, his long legs stretched out, smoking with one elbow on the table, and looking at the pleasure-boats that ply between the Old Port and the Château d'If, the island just outside the harbour.

'Have you been to the Château d'If?' he asked me.

'No.'

'Don't worry – I know people born here who've never set foot in the place.'

And there was I thinking that he was about to suggest taking me on the trip there. I don't know if he does it on purpose, but he can be baffling. There's an innocent look to him at times, just like a child. Is he married? To a white woman? He doesn't wear a wedding-ring. Mind you, a ring doesn't mean anything. Has he any children? I didn't put these questions to him; I checked myself in time. We got on to the subject – I don't know how – of the emigration of Africans to France. He knew plenty about that. As he talked, his tobacco-colour eyes took on a different shade. He spoke about them from the heart – the old men, the soldiers who were demobilized here, the seamen. He had a lot to say about the old ones especially, pitying them and taking their part. I had the air of a child listening to the complaints of an adult and being surprised that he should have any worries.

What age can he be? He has the bearing and vitality of a young man. (He said we'd have another drink, the same again, without asking me if I wanted one.) Then he decided it was time to go home. That made me miserable . . . the treat was over. We walked back. Do you think he asked if I was tired? No . . . .

When we reached my street door he said he would come and see me from time to time, and that if I wanted to see him urgently I had only to call at the Association's centre between six and seven.

If you saw him, you would approve. Oh, no doubt of it! He has already brought me the sunshine, the surf of the ocean of happiness. With him, everything has to be alive and genuine. Do you think I'm doing right? Of course, there's my condition. Will it be all right until the birth? I'm in raptures at seeing a gleam of life shining on the horizon at last.

That's all for now, old friend,
Nafi.

P.S. I've just counted the pages – there are ten. Too many.

... No, no! How do you expect me to follow your advice. He hasn't been back for four days. The last time he stayed until after midnight, and next morning my landlady gave me a dirty look. He sent another man to go with me to the Family Allowances office, saying that he was very busy. I'm waiting patiently for him to come and see me again. When will that be? He said to me the last time, 'I don't like your landlady.' But he didn't tell me why not.*

... Arona came to see me three days later. I heard his voice on the landing, through the skylight which I'd opened to have some air. He was talking to some Algerians, and I can still remember everything he said. He told the Algerians: 'If the FLN† gives orders that you're not to take part in the referendum, you'll have to obey. But we of Black Africa who work here, we must vote. Because our 'No' will have a double meaning. We'll be voting 'No' to show our solidarity with the French working class, for we benefit from the better conditions that they've gained by their struggles in the past, and also we're workers ourselves. Secondly, our 'No' will show that we want an end to colonial domination of our own country.'

He came to see me afterwards. But he didn't stay very long. He has to ...

* I came across these odd pages of letters, which I've gathered together here.
† The Algerian National Liberation Army. (Tr.)

· · · · ·

... at the risk of repeating myself, as in my previous letters, I still enjoy his company and conversation. I talk about all sorts of things with him – clothes, hair-styles, shoes, films ... He doesn't like Negresses – he always calls them that – who have the crinkle taken out of their hair. We've been to the shipping place together, then we bought a few things. Going down the main avenue, we laughed at everything. We had ourselves photographed. He'll go back to collect the photo. As we were walking along we saw a woman just in front of us with a little dog on a leash. 'Do you know what those dogs are called?' he whispered to me. I looked blank, showing him I'd no idea. 'Bum-lickers,' he said. I could feel the blood rush to my face, and didn't know where to put myself. This happened a second time when, in his free and easy way, he took me into a shop selling clothes for pregnant women.

He went up to the shopkeeper and said to him, 'My wife's expecting a baby, presumably mine, and would like a dress becoming to her condition of a gratified wife.' The shopkeeper looked me up and down. I felt confused and embarrassed. But with great tact – his slogan must be always be pleasant to customers – he replied, 'I'm very happy for you, sir, and for you too, madam.' Then he beckoned to a shopgirl to see to us. Arona, without giving her time to ask anything, said to her in the same tone as the shopkeeper had used, 'What colour will suit madam? As she's aubergine-black, I don't want anything too striking, but nothing neutral either.' I could have screamed; I felt like hitting him. What was I to do – walk out of the shop? Since meeting him, I can't control my nerves! While I was seething inwardly, he was feeling and examining the dresses, all with a straight face, holding them up to me and murmuring to the shopgirl, 'No, no, that won't do.' I'm not sure what happened after that, but when we were out in the street again he laughed and laughed. But I was furious. I'm not a clown. He doesn't care what I might think ... perhaps? But I don't think so.

The next thing was that he took me into a pastry-shop. There were quite a few people, about a dozen, waiting to be served. When our turn came, he asked for 'half-a-dozen Negro-lickers'. The woman behind the counter looked at me and blushed. And he, after staring at the poor woman, turned to me and said, 'Is that enough, darling?' You must admit, it was going a bit too far. And when we'd sat down at a table he said, 'I like a good laugh. But I don't often have the chance. So I take advantage of you being with me.' I didn't understand a word. I heard what he said all right, but what did he mean? However, my anger gradually subsided.

Him a hooligan? You're a long way out, dear. A man, yes – a combination of authority and vindictiveness, of a revolutionary and someone up to date. A stimulating person.

Well, we made a few more purchases. Oh, and then there's the film. When we got back he said, 'I'll call for you at half-past eight, to take you to the cinema.' No question of whether I was feeling well enough to go out again . . . No, he manages people as he decides on ways and means for them. I've had a glimpse of that.

So in the evening he took me to see *Limelight*. It's a Charlie Chaplin film. If you get the chance, if it comes to your town, do go and see it. It made me cry . . . the music and the dancing, and the dancer who trampled on the old man's feelings! Only someone inhuman could see this film without a tightening of the heart. Afterwards, walking back home from the cinema, he was silent. I concluded he was in one of his uncommunicative moods, and this led me to think over one or two things. Was it on purpose that he'd taken me to see this film? I asked him. For there was a similarity with my own situation.

'No,' he replied. 'You mean people are saying that I'm sleeping with you? Even that the child you're carrying is mine?'

I'd decided to risk everything, to bring matters to a head and put an end to this ambiguous situation between us. Never mind what the Africans here might think or would think. What do they know of my sufferings, of how low I've fallen? Haven't I the right to love, to laugh, to go out? No, of course not. They're all men, and men with conservative ideas, very reactionary. Quite a few of them abandoned their wives back in their own country two, three, even four years ago, and live here with white women. I had to take a strong hold on myself not to burst out in anger. 'And what do you think about these tales?' I asked him.

'What people are saying isn't true. And it makes my work more difficult.'

'How does it do that?'

He seemed not to have heard. His silence embarrassed me too much for me to repeat the question; I was torn between hoping he had not in fact heard and wanting a reply.

'Because I've no wish to take another man's wife,' he finally said.

'And supposing I was just any sort of woman?'

'I've no wish for any sort of woman either.'

'What you're doing or aiming at is more important?'

'For me, yes.'

'Is that why you take me around with you – for your own ends?'

'I don't see anything dishonest in that. If I need a woman, I pay for her.'

Beating him to death wouldn't have been good enough for him; stretching him out over an ant-heap, yes. I'd bared myself, I was naked, and he just pushed me aside, rejected me. We didn't exchange another word all the way back. I never want to see him again.

. . . My old man will be back in a few days. He's ill and in the sick-bay on board. It seems to be serious. Arona still comes just as he used to, and there's nothing in his look that recalls our argument after going to see that film. We haven't been to the cinema again. He's dealing with the forms for my admission to the maternity hospital.

As for my 'husband', my old man, he mentions in one of his letters the rumours going around among the Africans. But his letters are not so violent now as they were at first.

No, don't go to see a marabout. What for? Arona doesn't mean anything to me any more . . .

. . . You're badly mistaken. God knows I'd rather be mistaken than to have a moment's doubts. There's something that Madame

Baronne and Arona have in common. Madame Baronne is a Communist. 'A great-hearted woman,' my 'husband' once said of her. And indeed, she's the only woman I like talking with. She's lent me a magazine called *Femmes Françaises*. Everything is easy and straightforward with her. But some of her expressions escape me. Oh, the other day Arona came with a friend of his, who looked at the African-style garment I was wearing and said, 'African material is certainly pretty.' At which Arona commented, 'African material, stamped Boussac.' Who is Boussac? Madame Baronne told me – the biggest textile manufacturer in France.

It's odd, how deep your distrust goes. Thanks all the same.

. . . I'm at the maternity hospital. The Referendum has been held. Senegal has voted 'Yes'. It's odd. It's disappointing after the reception given to the General (De Gaulle). No one expected it – at least, not here. Here in France there's a majority for 'Yes'. Arona hasn't been to see me again. He must be taking his defeat badly. For his sake, I wanted the 'No' to win. My old 'husband' has been to see me though. He looks even more unpleasant than when he went away. I feel sorry for him. He's really very ill. He brought me a whole lot of things that he got on his voyage. He just sat near me, not saying a word, his head bowed as if the weight of years added to the burden of poverty crushed what dignity remains to him. The women in the ward with me thought that he's my father and that Arona is my husband. I was obliged to tell them they're wrong. What do you think the old man has? Cancer. His friends, those of his own generation, haven't come to see me. The reason? Arona. I'm all the better for it, anyway. I explained to the old man that there's never been anything between Arona and me. We're like brother and sister. He believes me – at least, that's what he says.

Everything is going well with me. I mean . . .

. . . Madame Baronne came to see me with her daughter. She brought me some bananas and said, 'These are fruit from your own country.' There's a student midwife here who's a Negress. From Togoland.

She came to see me too. Arona sent her. Can she be his fiancée?
The other women here are full of praise for her. She's a very hard
worker and the most conscientious of all the student nurses. She
gives me African newspapers to read. She comes twice a day.

I've two neighbours, the one in the bed on the left is an Arab,
she thinks I'm a Muslim; the one on the right is Italian, and she
thinks I'm a Roman Catholic.

I've nothing much to write to you about. I walk in the grounds
with some of the women. They make me laugh. They know nothing
at all about Africa. All day long I have to answer their daft questions.

Fond kisses, Nafi.

P.S. The old man is in a bad way, confined to his bed. I'm very
distressed about him.

Marseilles

My dear friend,

I've left hospital with a baby girl. A priest came to baptize her,
but I refused. She hasn't been baptized according to Muslim rites
either, nor to those of our country. She's been named after the old
man's mother – Yaye Codou. So now I'm back in my pigeon-hole . . .
It's lucky that the old man is in hospital, for with a baby weighing
all of six pounds the room would be much too small. Three of us
in this match-box – it's just not possible. I must find somewhere
else to live. In this room that's twelve feet square there's a double
bed, a wardrobe, some suitcases, sacks of kola-nuts and all my
cooking things. To make a little space, I've taken the baby's pram
to pieces. She's in the bed with me.

I've had a letter from my father. He sends me advice and encour-
agement and talks about a wife being submissive, a sort of unobtru-
sive shadow. It's very easy to give advice and tell me what to do.
I don't hold it against him – my father I mean – he's only conforming
to type. The times are changing but he can't see it and he still
clings to his old-fashioned ideas. Mother hasn't written at all.

Do you remember what we used to say about the first baby we'd
have – my first this and that? The reality is turning out to be quite

different. It's very hard for me – I don't know what to compare my situation with. All I know is that our dreams resulted from a sort of torpor of the mind, that we were much too sensitive and influenced by the life around us. Almost as if we were drugged.

I don't like France. What is France to me, anyway? These four walls, that's all!

Madame Baronne comes to see me nearly every day. She tells me that I'm wasting away, and I can well believe her. She must have guessed how lonely I am; she keeps inviting me, but I don't want to go. She knows I'm alone, very much alone just now, without relatives, friends or neighbours. There's no neighbourliness in this country. I'm a stranger here. The women I sometimes meet down at the shipping place, seeing me with Yaye Codou, say, 'Oh, what a lovely baby! A boy?' 'No, a girl,' I reply. 'Oh, I'd have said a boy,' they say. And that's all. My black neighbours are worse than the white.

This is a letter from me to you alone.

Yours ever, Nafi.

My mind was made up before going to see my old man. I'd done all my packing and I was going to tell him I was leaving. I can't stand it any longer. I've had enough! This room! With this baby! And all alone! I couldn't go on. But when I got to the hospital and went into the ward and saw him lying there, his face all drawn and his breathing so harsh, I couldn't hold back my tears. There were some of his old friends at his bedside. They sit with him, watch over him with faces like death-masks. It's the final mark of their affection for him. They all know he's had it. I was sitting at the back and saying over to myself, 'Demba, I've made up my mind, I'm going back to the old country.' But it was impossible for me to say that out loud – I just couldn't. Yet I can't wait until his end comes. When will that be? Tomorrow – or not for a year or two?

No one could make the decision for me. There they were, his old companions, calmly convinced of approaching death. Which will be the next to go? I'd rather it were one of them and not me. They've had their life. Mine is still ahead of me. Looking at them gives me indigestion for this life. What has happened to my insatiable appetite for life?

The words suddenly slipped from me, automatically: 'Demba, I'm going back home.' What else could I do? Nothing . . . I think the old man moved . . . an arm. But that was all. The others were still staring at the same spot. Not one of them had looked up at me. I was in a cold sweat. I was expecting some response, but none came. God knows I don't refuse to watch over him. God knows that! But I'm unable to, here. A woman left alone, with a young baby to look after, never any sun for her nappies and other things. This damp room which never gets a single ray of sunshine. It'll be the death of me! No, I can't stay here – they can think what they like. Stay and wait for him to get better? He never will get better. He wanted a young wife to end his days with. I don't want to die – not here. It's enough to drive you mad. The baby crying . . . And those yells! I lost all taste for things a long while ago. I haven't even time to attend to myself. When I look in a mirror I don't recognize myself. It's a martyrdom – and all because of a photograph.

In his last letter my father talked of God. It's not a question of Him, but of me – me, very much alive. I've stopped replying to father's letters. It's better that way. One of these fine mornings he'll see me arrive. When I left I was just a child – in my mind – but I'm not any longer.

I left the hospital ward soon afterwards. None of them got up to see me out.

Arona came to see me. 'There's nothing I can say – nothing I can say to you,' were his words. He doesn't approve of me. Not in the slightest. But I don't give a damn for his ideas, big or little. 'Where will you get the money for your ticket home?' he asked. I hadn't thought about that. The swine, they've really got me. Arona had thought about it – but in which way? I've no idea, and he'll probably never tell me. Nobody will come to my aid, I told Arona. Then I shouted that I didn't like France. He smiled slightly and said, 'You know nothing about France.'

My very dear friend,

What would have happened to me if it weren't for you? My one support, the only person I could confide in. You'll never know just how much our correspondence has meant to me. Without this coming and going of letters I should have been cut off from my source, been lost and gone astray. I'm no poet, but I wish I could write and make you feel all my emotions. Despite all the water between us, our exchanges have put the seal on our friendship.

Well, it's all over! My 'husband' is dead. Dead, I tell you. A fortnight ago. He was given a fine funeral. The whole of the African colony attended. I was there too – which is against all tradition. Arona said to me that if I wanted to go, I could, after all. That 'after all' grieved me. It was full of reproach. The other day he told me: 'I've a lot of admiration for our elders – the old men here. They've never wanted to become neutral and assimilate with the French. They've remained Africans in the true sense of the word.' But what does it matter to me, what Arona or any of them thinks. To him, the end justifies the means. He spares nobody and never forgives anyone. As for the others, let's say no more about them.

The death of the old man distresses me, just a little. I should be telling you a lie if I said the opposite. And another thing – I'm letting my thoughts run on, I'm so happy – I shan't have to go into mourning. The elders had a meeting to decide about it. I had to admire Arona's coolness and clarity. That man is capable of killing a baby in support of his ideas. He stood up for me, even though he disapproves of my conduct. He took a realistic view in fact. It was after they'd all left that I thought over and admired what he'd said to the others. 'She can't stay shut up for forty days, seeing no one but her close relatives,' he put it to them. 'And who is her close relative here? Who is there to go to market for her? A wife in mourning in our country is not allowed to go out, must not see any men nor even talk to them, except through a thick screen. She has to be kept from temptation, guarded against the weakness of the flesh. Demba's widow ought to be sent back home as soon as possible. That's my opinion on the matter.' After a long discussion, the others agreed with him. And the more I think about it, the more I wish it. And I can understand their situation in France, too.

I've settled all my affairs here, as well as those of my dead husband, and I shall be taking ship in a fortnight's time.

This is my last letter from France.

Good-bye for now, dear, and I'll tell you the rest when I see you.

Yours ever,
Nafi.

9
The Community

In olden times when men and beasts spoke to each other, the animals used to hold their own meetings. As cats were living with men, or rather have always lived with us, they embraced the Faith. But the Faith makes demands, which often call for a great deal of effort, both of mind and resources. El Hadj Niara, the cat, undertook a great preaching campaign on his return from Mecca, with the object of converting all the rats and founding a large community. He began by sending an emissary to address the *dieunahs* (the rats).

'I bring you the respectful greetings of our revered Iman, El Hadj Niara,' began the envoy, surrounded by a crowd of tempting rodents. 'He has charged me to say that on Friday next you are bidden to gather under the big tree in Abada-Thioye Square. As you know, he has just returned from the Holy City, and he would like you to have the benefit of hearing his views on the dangers of the present time, to facilitate your entry into the great community, and to read to you from the Holy Book.'

'Go back and tell him that we have heard his grievances and that we thank him. *Inch' Allah*, we will be there on the appointed day,' replied Inekeiv (this name does not quite mean sly or cunning, but the two combined).

The envoy departed. Inekeiv was thoughtful for a while, then he said to the other rats:

'My grandfather was eaten by the *mousses* (cats). His grandfather was, too. So were my grandchildren. I do not mistrust titles, nor do I doubt his good faith, but the name of the tree alone, Abada-Thioye, makes me feel uneasy – it means a tree-trunk with no end to it. We'd have to go on running until death overtook us. And what's this community?'

'Oh, the young ones are beginning to cry,' exclaimed a few old rats.

'Let him finish,' shouted the young ones.

'As we ought to go to this gathering, and as the elders have agreed to this community, let us dig runs from our dwellings to the tree. It will then be easier for us to escape if the need arises.'

The applause of some and the demonstrations of others caused Inekeiv to bring his speech to an end.

On the Friday there were a large number of cats on the fringe of the prayer-meeting, surrounding the *dieunahs*. El Hadj Niara made his appearance in a garment edged with gold, the hood of a large burnous over his head, and his old *babouches* flapping with every step he took; he was telling his beads in a dignified way. The cats and the rats looked at him in wonder. Perched on a bench, the preacher began with the words with which every chapter in the Koran opens.

'In the name of Allah, the compassionate and the merciful . . . I thank you for coming in such numbers. The peace of God be with you . . .'

'Amen, amen,' they responded.

'Before going any further, I should like to warn you of certain facts. For instance, it is forbidden by religion to gnaw the feet of sleeping people, for it causes the victims to stay in bed for some days! Another thing – what cannot be measured must not spoil what can be measured. Men do not spend a lot of money on clothes for you to make holes in them. That also is forbidden.'

Inekeiv, who was listening attentively with his nose pointing upwards and his short tail curled round, spoke up sharply:

'El Hadj, in the Holy Book it is surely also written that there is greater sorrow for a woman who comes home to find her children devoured than to see clothes with holes in them. I have not been to Mecca, but that is surely forbidden. And what have you to say about the dismay of men who have had nothing to eat all day and arrive home at night expecting to eat their meagre supper, but instead find nothing. Is not that also a sin, to gobble up other people's possessions?'

The assembly, that is to say the *dieunahs*, began to feel ill at ease. It was no longer a friendly meeting. The tom-cat El Hadj Niara became annoyed; however, he concealed it and continued with even greater ardour. 'Religion punishes all those who nibble or gnaw at food stocks! All those who attack the feet of sleeping people . . .'

'Why, El Hadj, do you say nothing against those who play about with snakes and instead of killing them put them in men's beds, with the likelihood that the poor devils will be bitten and die soon afterwards? I have not been to the Kaâba, but surely that also is forbidden. As for the community . . .'

'I can see that you're just trying to contradict me,' exclaimed El Hadj, most displeased. 'Go for the infidels!' he ordered his followers.

The fight and scuffle that ensued raised clouds of dust. The few rats who had heeded Inekeiv's words and made runs to the tree were able to scramble to safety; but the following day many *dieunahs* were missing.

Since that time, *dieunahs* have refused to accept any religion or to join any community. And it is since then that they have always made runs for themselves.

Personally, I am reminded of that *Communauté Rénovée.**

* Name given to the French Community overseas after its Constitution was revised. This was the alternative to Independence. (Tr.)

10

Chaiba the Algerian

There seemed to be no flesh on his body, and the skin was stretched tight over the bones of his face; his thin-lipped mouth had deep lines on either side, and his hair had receded from his narrow fore-head. But he had mischievous, laughing eyes, dark grey, with thick lashes and eyebrows. His colour was not the dark tan that racialists usually associate with all North African Arabs, but was more like the subdued shade that the African soil takes on at twilight and at dawn. He walked bent slightly forward, as though his back pained him; and owing to a deformed spine he leaned to the right, which made his right arm seem longer than his left. He wore a red flannel body-belt, as did all the stevedores of his generation.

He worked in the port of Marseilles, which was where I met him. When he first joined the gang I worked in, to replace a man who had been hurt the day before, I was filled with pity for him. He was only half a man, I said to myself. And Chaiba was proud; he had that absurd pride which makes humble men always want to pit themselves against something stronger than themselves.

He told me later that he had been working in the Marseilles docks for nearly twenty-five years. Twenty-five years as a stevedore, and always working down in the hold. He became my mate, and through-out the long shifts, over the weeks and months, he proved to be the best partner I have ever had. He had more experience than I, and knew at a glance just where to put a packing-case, and whether it should be stood upright or on its side. We acted as one, had the same ideas about handling a crate, whether to roll or lift it; without saying a word we knew the right place to put it, and with just a look we fitted it in there neatly. (I don't know whether you've ever worked as a stevedore, but there are some men who fit in well with you, whose ways of doing things match your own, and this is important.) Chaiba was one such; we often laughed about it, saying it was as though we were married.

He came from the Aurès, the mountainous region south of Constantine, but he rarely talked about his native village or his homeland. His wife and children had joined him. He liked some aspects of France but had a deep hatred of the caids and the colonists. I never discovered why, however. He liked his snuff; when he took a pinch, his eyes twinkled under their long lashes. A favourite subject of his was the cinema. On Sundays he took his whole family to see a film. He always went to the same cinema, in the rue des Dominicaines. It was the only one where Arab films were shown. Afterwards, they all went back home – to a furnished room.

He worked hard, doing overtime to send some money to help his relatives in Algeria. We were walking home at six o'clock one morning, at the end of a sixteen-hour shift. Another docker, a European, was with us. Just as we reached the Colbert post office, a police patrol on bicycles stopped us. After checking our identity-cards, they took Chaiba away with them. He was detained for three days. Why? From that time, never a week passed without the police questioning him. As if some disease were eating him away, gradually rotting his whole body, Chaiba became increasingly morose and hardly ever spoke a word. He stopped going to the cinema with his family.

A few days ago, while in Dakar, I saw in a newspaper that Chaiba had been deported, had been put in an internment camp, had tried to escape while armed with a weapon, and been shot dead.

The Algerian War of Independence had been on for six years. I never knew what Chaiba's ideas and feelings were on that subject. He was fully entitled to hate caids and colonists if he wished. He was not an extremist and certainly not a revolutionary. But he had been born in Algeria. His colour was that of the African soil at twilight. He loved his wife and children, went to the cinema once a week to see Arab films, liked his snuff . . . All that did not make a revolutionary of him.

But perhaps he believed that dignity and the respect of his children could only be acquired at the cost of a certain kind of life.

Chaiba was a friend. I am proud to think that he was a friend, with his colour like that of the African soil at dawn – a new dawn for Africa.

II

The Promised Land

On this morning in late June 1958 the thoughts of the people in two cars speeding towards Antibes were not on the fate of the French Republic nor on the future of Algeria, nor on the other territories under the colonial yoke. The two cars turned into the Chemin de l'Ermitage, then stopped with a shriek of brakes. The men jumped out and walked swiftly up the gravel drive of a villa. To the left of the villa was the open door of a garage; a weather-worn panel gave the name of the villa – Le Bonheur Vert. The leading man was the examining magistrate of Grasse, the administrative centre of this area bordering the Mediterranean; he was followed by a police doctor, two inspectors and a couple of policemen.

The only thing green about Le Bonheur Vert was its name. The formal garden had gravel paths that curved round two palm-trees with drooping leaves. The examining magistrate stopped to gaze at the front of the villa, noting the window with its broken pane and the ladder leaning against the wall.

Inside the villa were several other police inspectors, a police photographer, and some men who appeared to be journalists; these last were gazing idly at the African statuettes, the masks, skins of wild animals and ostrich eggs which were displayed here and there. On entering the living-room the new arrivals had the impression of penetrating a hunter's den.

Two women were sitting there, sobbing. They were very much alike, having the same narrow forehead and arched nose; and now their dark-ringed eyes were red from weeping.

'After my siesta, I felt like having a bath,' the one in the light dress began to tell the examining magistrate. 'The bathroom door was locked from the inside (she blew her nose). I thought it must be the maid having a bath. I say "the maid",' she explained, 'but we always called her by her name – Diouana. I waited for over an hour, but I didn't see her come out. So I went back. I called, I tried the door, but it was still locked. And there was no sound from inside. So then I called our neighbour, the captain here . . .'

She stopped and wiped her nose, then began weeping again. Her sister, who was younger and had her hair cut short, bent towards her.

The magistrate turned to the man. 'It was you who found the body?'

'Yes. Well, when Madame called me, saying that the black woman had locked herself in the bathroom, I thought it was some sort of a joke. I was in the navy for thirty-five years, you know. I've sailed all the oceans. But I'm retired now.'

'Yes, yes. We know that, captain.'

'Well, when Madame called me, I brought my ladder along.'

'So it was you who thought of the ladder?'

'Well, it was Mademoiselle, Madame's sister, who suggested that I should bring it. When I climbed up to the window, I saw the black woman lying in a pool of blood.'

'Where is the key of the door?'

'I have it, sir,' said the inspector.

'I only wanted to see it.'

'I've looked at the window,' said the other inspector.

'I opened it after breaking the pane,' said the retired sailor.

'Which pane did you break?'

'Which pane?' repeated the old sea-dog. (He was wearing white linen trousers and a blue jacket.)

'Yes. I've seen it, but I'd like you to tell me exactly.'

'The second pane from the top,' Mademoiselle replied for him.

Just then two men came down the stairs with a stretcher on which lay a body covered with a blanket. Blood was dripping on to the stairs. The magistrate stepped forward and lifted a corner of the blanket. He frowned as he looked down at a black woman with her throat cut from ear to ear.

'It was done with this knife. A kitchen knife,' said a man at the top of the stairs.

'Did you bring her back with you from Africa or did you engage her here?'

'We brought her from Africa, in April this year,' the elder woman replied. 'She came by sea. My husband is employed by Dakar Aeronautics, and the company only gives free transport to our family. She had been with us in Dakar for two and a half years, or it might be three.'

'How old was she?'

'I don't know exactly.'

'According to her identity-card she was born in 1927.'

'Oh, the natives don't know their date of birth,' put in the retired captain, thrusting his hands into his pockets.

'I can't think why she killed herself. She was well treated here; she ate what we did, and slept in the same room as my children.'

'Where is your husband?'

'He went to Paris the day before yesterday.'

'Ah!' said the inspector, still gazing round at the ornaments. 'Why do you think it was suicide?'

'Why?' echoed the captain. 'Oh, who do you think is going to take the life of a black woman? She never went out. She knew nobody, except Madame's children.'

The newspaper reporters were becoming impatient. A servant's suicide, even though she was a black, would never make the front page. It was not a sensation.

'I think she was homesick,' said the wife. 'A change came over her in recent weeks, and she was quite peculiar.'

The examining magistrate went upstairs with an inspector. They examined the bathroom and the window, while the others waited down below.

'You will be informed when the doctor has completed his examination,' the inspector told the wife and her sister when he came down again.

He and the examining magistrate then left together; they had been barely an hour at the villa. The others followed them; the cars and the ambulance sped away, leaving the two women to their thoughts.

The wife's mind went back to her charming villa just outside Dakar. She saw Diouana pushing open the gate, telling the Alsatian to stop barking . . .

It all began out there in Africa. Three times a week Diouana used to trudge the four miles there and back. But for the past month she had been happy and gay, her heart beating as though she had fallen in love. The road was long between her home and her employers' villa. On the outskirts of Dakar was a spread of new houses in a flowery setting of cacti, bougainvillaea and jasmine, and the asphalted Avenue Gambetta stretched ahead like a long black ribbon. The little housemaid no longer cursed this road and her employers as in the past. It was a long way to walk, but for the past month it had not seemed so, not since Madame had said she would take her to France. The name 'France' constantly hammered in her mind. All living things around her had become ugly, and the splendid villas she had admired so often now seemed shabby.

In order to travel, to go to France, she needed an identity-card, as she came from the Upper Casamance. It took the whole of her scanty savings. That doesn't matter, she said to herself, I'm going to France.

'Is that you, Diouana?'

'Yes, Madame,' she answered as she entered the hall, looking neat in her light dress and with her straight hair carefully combed.

'Good. The master has gone into town. Go and look after the children.'

'Yes, Madame,' she said in her childish voice.

Diouana was not quite thirty; on her identity-card her year of birth was given as 1927. She must have been of age. She went to find the children. In all the rooms there were crates and bundles;

everything was packed, tied up and ready. There was little left for
Diouana to do. For the past ten days she had been washing clothes
and linen. Strictly speaking, that was her function – a washerwoman.
The family had three servants; a cook, a kitchen-boy and herself.

'Diouana . . . Diouana.' Madame was calling her.

'Yes, Madame?' she answered, coming out of the children's
bedroom.

Notebook in hand, Madame was checking all the luggage once
again. The men should be coming to collect it at any moment.

'Have you seen your family? Do you think they'll be pleased?'

'Yes, Madame. All very glad. I ask mama for me, ask papa
Boutoupa too,' she said.

Her eyes, glowing with pleasure, gazed at the bare wall. Her
heart almost stopped beating. She could not bear it if Madame
changed her mind. The joy went from her ebony-black face as she
looked down, prepared to implore her mistress to take her.

'I don't want you to let me down at the last minute.'

'No, Madame. Me go. Go to France!'

The two were thinking about it in very different ways. Diouana
wanted to visit France and return home from that country so
renowned for its beauty, wealth and pleasant living. You made
your fortune there. Already, even before leaving African soil, she
could see herself on the quayside, just back from France, rolling in
money and with clothes for everyone. She dreamed of the freedom
she would have to go where she wanted, of not having to work
like a horse. She could not bear it if Madame refused to take
her.

Madame remembered her last leave in France, three years before.
She had only two children then. In Africa, she had acquired bad
habits in her attitude towards servants. When she had engaged a
housemaid in France, not only were the wages high but the maid
even insisted upon a day off each week. She had been obliged to
dismiss her and engage another. The second was no different from
the first; worse, in fact. That young woman had even stood up to
her, saying 'If you are able to have children, you ought to be able

to look after them yourself. I'll do the housework, but I'm not going to live in. I've got my own children to look after, and my husband too.'

It had been a great change from being waited on hand and foot. Instead of having a holiday, she had found herself with burdensome family duties. Soon she was urging her husband to return to Africa.

Back in Dakar, tired out and deeply annoyed, her pride wounded, she had laid plans for the next leave. She advertised for a housemaid in all the papers. About a hundred girls came in reply. Her choice fell upon Diouana, who had just arrived in Dakar from her 'native bush'; and for three years she kept dangling the trip to France before Diouana's eyes. For three thousand francs a month – a miserly wage by European standards – any African girl would have followed her to the ends of the earth. As an additional bait, when the time of departure drew near, she gave Diouana a few extra coins now and again, or some old clothes and worn-out shoes.

Such was the unbridgeable gulf that separated the maid from her mistress.

'You've given your identity-card to the master?'

'Yes, Madame.'

'Go on with your work then. Tell the cook to get a good meal for the three of you.'

'Thank you, Madame,' Diouana answered, and went to the kitchen.

Her mistress continued checking the luggage.

The husband returned at midday, his arrival being announced by the dog's barking. He found his wife still with pencil in hand. 'Isn't the van there yet, to take our luggage?' she asked irritably.

'It's coming at a quarter to two. Our things will go aboard last of all, on top of the others', so we shall have them first at Marseilles. Where's Diouana? Diouana!'

The eldest of the children ran to fetch her. She was under the trees with the baby.

'Yes, Madame?'

'The master wants to see you.'

D

'It's all fixed up,' he told her. 'Here are your ticket and your identity-card.'

Diouana held out her hand to take them.

'Keep your identity-card, and I'll take care of the ticket. The Duponts are going back by ship and they'll look after you. Are you pleased to be going to France?'

'Yes, Missie (the nearest she could get to Monsieur).'

'Good! Where's your luggage?'

'At home, rue Escarfait, Missie.'

'Right. I'll just have lunch, then I'll take you in the car.'

'Bring the children in, Diouana, it's time for their siesta.'

'Yes, Madame.'

Diouana did not feel hungry. The kitchen-boy, who was two years younger than her, kept going noiselessly between dining-room and kitchen, taking full plates and bringing away the empty ones. The cook was perspiring freely. He was not feeling happy, for he would soon be out of work; this, for him, was the consequence of his employers' departure for France. And for that reason, he bore a grudge against the maid. But Diouana, looking out of the big window with its wide view of the sea, was mentally following the birds flying high over the vast blue expanse. The offshore island of Gorea was only just visible. She turned her identity-card over and over in her hand, looking at it and smiling to herself. She was not quite satisfied with the photograph; it did not stand out clearly enough. But never mind, she thought, I'm going, and that is what matters.

'Samba,' said the master, coming into the kitchen. 'We've had an excellent meal today. You really surpassed yourself. The mistress is very pleased with you.'

The kitchen-boy had straightened himself; the cook put a hand to his tall white toque and tried to raise a smile.

'Thank you very much, Missie,' he said. 'Me pleased too, very pleased, because Missie and Madame pleased. Missie very kind. My family very sad. Missie gone, me no work.'

'We'll be back again, poor old boy. Anyway, you'll find work, a good cook like you.'

Samba was not so sure. The whites are stingy, he knew well. And Dakar was swarming with up-country people claiming to be accomplished cooks, so it was not easy to find a job, he thought.

'We'll be back, Samba. Sooner than you think, perhaps. The last time we only stayed two and a half months.'

These consoling remarks came from the mistress, who had just joined her husband in the kitchen, and to them Samba could but reply, 'Thank you, Madame. Madame, good lady.'

Madame was pleased, too. She knew from experience what it meant to have a good reputation among the servant class.

'You can finish at four o'clock, and the master will take you back to town with him then. I'll pack the rest of the luggage. When we come back to Dakar, I promise I'll take you on again. Does that satisfy you?'

'Thank you, Madame.'

She and her husband left the kitchen, and Samba gave Diouana a playful slap; she turned to retaliate.

'Hey, steady on! You're going away today. We mustn't end up by having a scrap.'

'You hurt me,' she said.

'And what about Missie? Doesn't he hurt you?'

Samba suspected there was something between the master and Diouana.

'They're calling you, Diouana. I can hear the car.'

She went off without even saying good-bye.

The car sped along the main road. It was not often that Diouana had the honour of being driven by the master. Her eyes implored the pedestrians to look at her, not daring to wave to them or call out 'I'm off to France'. Yes, France. She was convinced that her pleasure must be evident to all. The hidden springs of her bubbling joy were throwing her off balance. When the car drew up in front of the house in the rue Escarfait she was taken aback. 'So soon,' she said to herself. To the right of their modest house, a few men were drinking at tables outside the bar *Le Gai Navigateur*, and four others were standing on the pavement having a quiet talk.

'So you're off today, little cousin?' said Tive Correa, swaying drunkenly, his legs astride and holding a bottle by its neck. His clothes were shabby and crumpled.

Diouana refused to listen to him; she had no need of advice from a drunkard. She hurried into the house. Tive Correa was an old sailor who had returned from Europe after being away for twenty years. He had sailed away in the fullness of his youth, bursting with ambition, and had returned a wreck of a man. He had wanted all that life could offer, and had brought back nothing but an immoderate love of the bottle. He prophesied nothing but woe. Diouana had asked his advice, and he had been against her going to France.

He took a few hesitant steps towards the car, still clutching his bottle.

'Is it true that she's going to France with you, Monsieur?'

Monsieur made no reply. He lit a cigarette, and as he blew the smoke out of the window he looked Tive Correa up and down. The man really was a poor specimen in his greasy clothes, smelling of palm wine.

'I lived in France for twenty years,' Tive said with a trace of pride in his voice, leaning a hand on the car door. 'You see me like this, but I know France better than you do. During the war I was living in Toulon, and when the Germans arrived they sent me and other Africans to Aix-en-Provence, to work in the Gardanne mines. I was against Diouana going to France.'

'We didn't force her, did we? She wants to go,' Monsieur coldly retorted.

'Of course. Is there any young African who doesn't long to go to France? Alas, the youngsters don't know the difference between living in France and being a servant there. We come from neighbouring villages in Upper Casamance, Diouana and me. There, we don't say as you do that the light attracts moths; where I live in the

Casamance country we say that it's the darkness that drives the moths away.'

Just then, Diouana came out of the house with several women. They were chattering away, each asking her to bring back a little souvenir. Diouana promised gaily, smiling and showing her white teeth.

'The others are down at the quayside,' said one. 'Don't forget about a dress for me.'

'I should like shoes for the children. I've put the sizes in your suitcase. Remember to get a sewing-machine.'

'And some nice slips for me.'

'Write and tell me the price of irons for getting the crinkle out of hair, and I'd like a red jacket with big buttons, size forty-four.'

'Don't forget to send some money to your mother and Boutoupa.'

They all had something to tell her, to ask her to get. Diouana promised everything, her face beaming. Tive Correa picked up her case and pushed her into the car with a drunken but not unkind movement.

'Let her get away, women! D'you think money is easy to come by in France? She'll be able to tell you a thing or two when she comes back.'

'O . . . Oh!' the women shrieked at him.

'Good-bye, little cousin. Look after yourself. You have the address of your cousin in Toulon. Write to him as soon as you can. He'll be useful to know. Let me kiss you.'

Monsieur was growing impatient; he revved up the engine as a polite way of indicating that he'd had enough and it was time to go.

The car drove off to much waving of arms. At the quayside there was a repetition of it all – friends and relatives crowded round her to say farewell and give her instructions as to what to bring back, while Monsieur hovered impatiently in the background. At last he saw her on board.

She had a week at sea. Nothing to report, she would have written if she had kept a diary – and if she had been able to read and write.

There was just the sea in front and behind, to port and to starboard, just a watery sheet and the sky above.

Monsieur was there waiting for her when she landed and had completed the formalities. He drove fast towards the Riviera. Her eyes took everything in and she gazed in wonder and admiration. Her mind became filled with these first impressions. How beautiful it was! Africa now seemed no more than a sordid slum. The coast road led through one town after another, with a stream of buses, cars and lorries in both directions. This dense traffic amazed her.

'Did you have a good passage?'

'Yes, Missie,' she would have answered if he had asked.

They arrived at Antibes after a two hours' drive.

The days and weeks had gone by and Diouana was starting on her third month. She was no longer a lively, laughing young woman. Her eyes were sunken and dulled, and her glance failed to take things in. She had far more work to do than ever she had in Africa. She was eating her heart out, and her old friends would hardly have recognized her. France, beautiful France, was but a vague image, a fleeting vision; all she knew of it was the unkempt garden, the evergreen hedges of the other villas, and their roofs poking up above the green trees and palm-trees. Everyone seemed to live his own life, shut away in his house. Her master and mistress often went out, leaving her with the four children. They had soon ganged up against her and were always plaguing her. You must keep them amused, Madame said. The eldest, a cheeky lad, brought in others of his kind and they played at being explorers; Diouana was the 'savage'. The children tormented her. Sometimes the eldest was given a good hiding. He had picked up ideas about racial discrimination without properly understanding them, from hearing his parents talking with their neighbours in Africa, and now he gave his young friends a magnified version of them. Unknown to his parents, they would spring out on Diouana and run round her, chanting:

'There's the Negress,
There's the Negress,
Black as the darkest night.'

This persecution preyed upon her mind. At Dakar, the problem
of the colour of her skin had never arisen. But the children's baiting
caused her to think about it, and she realized that here she was not
only quite alone, but she had nothing in common with others. And
this made her feel ill, it infected her whole life and the air she
breathed.

Everything became blurred, dissolved and vanished – the life she
had dreamed about, the happiness she had thought to have. She was
worked off her feet. She was cook, nursemaid and laundress all in
one. Madame's sister had come to stay at the villa, so there were
seven people to look after. When she was at last able to go up to
bed, she fell asleep at once and slept like a log.

Venom entered her heart; she had never had any reason to hate
people before. Everything became monotonous and dreary. She
wondered where France was – the France of the fine cities she had
seen on the screen in Dakar cinemas, of delicious food and dense
crowds? The people of France were reduced to these unkind brats
and to Monsieur, Madame and Mademoiselle, who had become
strangers to her. The whole country contracted to the boundaries of
the villa. Slowly but surely, she was sinking under it all. Her wide
outlook in the past was narrowed down to the colour of her skin,
which suddenly instilled her with terror. Her skin; her blackness.
Fearfully, she took refuge within herself.

Her mind ran on the subject; but as there was no one with whom
she could exchange ideas, she talked to herself for hours on end.

One day her mistress had cunningly coaxed her to go and cook
lunch for them all at her parents' home in Cannes.

'We're going to Cannes tomorrow. My parents have never tasted
African cooking. You'll be a credit to us Africans,' Madame had
said while sunbathing almost naked in the garden.

'Yes, Madame.'

'I've ordered some rice and two chickens. But don't put in too much spice.'

'No, Madame,' she replied, her heart heavy within her.

This would not be the first time by any means that she had been lugged out to someone's villa to do the cooking. It was at the house of the 'Captain' – as everyone called him – that she had first rebelled. He had invited to dinner some gushing people who came out to the kitchen, watched what she was doing and got in her way. Their presence was a pestering shadow to her every movement, making her feel that she did not know how to do anything. These selfish and sophisticated people never stopped asking her idiotic questions on how black women did their cooking. She had to make a great effort to control herself.

Even while she served at table, the three women had still twittered away about the food; they had tasted it suspiciously, then greedily devoured the lot.

'You must do your very best this time, at my parents'.'

'Yes, Madame.'

She went back into the kitchen and thought how kind her mistress had been to her in the past, in Dakar. She loathed that kindness now. It had been induced by self-interest; its only reason had been to bind her, to lay a claim to her, in order to get the utmost out of her later. She loathed everything. In Dakar she used to wrap up the food that her employers left and take it back to the rue Escarfait, and she had been proud of working for the 'Grand Whites'. Now their food revolted her, in her loneliness. These feelings and this resentment affected and spoilt her relations with her employers. She kept to her place, they to theirs. No words passed between them except what was strictly necessary.

'Diouana, I want you to do the washing today.'

'Yes, Madame.'

'Right. Go up and fetch my slips and Missie's shirts.'

Later it would be, 'Diouana, I want you to do the ironing this afternoon.'

'Yes, Madame.'

'Last time you ironed my slips badly. The iron was too hot. Missie's shirt-collars were scorched, too. You really must pay attention to what you're doing.'

'Yes, Madame.'

'Oh, I was forgetting – some buttons need sewing on Missie's shirt and trousers.'

She had to do everything. Moreover, Madame usually said 'Missie' to her, even in front of guests. In order to make herself understood, she used the same jargon as the maid; it was the only thing she was honest about. The whole household ended up by referring to the maid as 'Missie'. Bewildered by her small knowledge of French, Diouana withdrew into herself even more. She ruminated over her situation and came to the conclusion that she was nothing but a useful object and that her employers showed her off as if she were some trophy or other. When they had guests in for the evening they sometimes talked about the psychology of the 'natives', and took her as an example. The neighbours called her 'their black servant'. But she was not black to herself, and that wounded her.

As time passed, everything got worse and she saw more clearly. She had more work than she could cope with, from one week's end to the next. The Lord's Day was Mademoiselle's favourite time for inviting her friends, and the house became filled with them. One week ended with them, and the next began with them.

It was all quite plain to her now. Why had Madame been so anxious for her to come? There had been calculation behind the gifts and the little extras. Madame no longer looked after the children; she kissed them when they got up in the morning, and that was all. And what had happened to that beautiful France? Diouana had seen nothing of it. These questions kept going through her mind. I'm cook, nursemaid and chambermaid, I do all the washing and iron it, and all for a pittance, three thousand francs a month. I do the work of six people. So why am I here?

Diouana became immersed in her memories. She compared her native bush to this dead brushwood around her. What a difference between these trees and her Casamance forest, so far away! The

memory of her village and the communal life there made her feel
more cut off than ever. She bit her lip and deeply regretted having
come. A thousand and one details flashed through her mind as she
looked back at the past.

She became aware again of the present, of the reality of her life in
France, where she was doubly a foreigner, and her mind hardened.
She thought of Tive Correa, not for the first time; his words were
proving only too true, cruelly so. She would have liked to write to
him, but could not. She had only had two letters from her mother
since her arrival in France. She had no time to reply, although
Madame had promised to write for her. But was it possible to say to
Madame all that went through her mind? She was angry with herself, for her ignorance silenced her. This impotence on her part
made her foam with rage. Moreover, Mademoiselle had taken her
stamps.

However, a pleasant thought crossed her mind and brought a
smile to her lips. That evening, Monsieur was sitting alone in front
of the television. She took advantage, went and stood where
Madame could not help seeing her, then left the room.

'Sold, sold . . . bought, bought,' she said to herself over and over
again. 'I've been bought, I do all the work here for three thousand
francs. I was enticed here, bound, and now I'm chained here like a
slave.'

She knew the real facts now. Later in the evening she opened her
suitcase, looked at all the things in it and wept. No one bothered
about her.

Still, she went on with her daily chores, the same routine, but
remained as close as an oyster at low tide in the Casamance river
back home.

'Douna,' called Mademoiselle. Of course, she could not possibly
say 'Di-ou-a-na.'

That made her still more wrathful. Mademoiselle was even lazier
than Madame, with her 'Come and take this away' – 'There's that
to be done, Douna' – 'Why don't you get on with this, Douna?' –
'You could rake the garden over now and again, Douna.' To this,

Diouana gave a fiery look for reply. Madame complained to her husband, who promised to have a word with the maid.

'What's the matter, Diouana? Are you ill or what?' he asked.

Still slaving away, she remained silent.

'You can tell me if there's anything wrong. Perhaps you'd like to go to Toulon. I haven't had the time yet, but we could go tomorrow.'

'Anyone would think she loathes us,' remarked Madame.

Three days after this incident, Diouana had a bath. Madame returned from a walk and then had a nap; afterwards she went to the bathroom but quickly came out again, calling for the maid.

'Diouana, you really are dirty! You might have left the bathroom clean and tidy.'

'Not me, Madame. The children, yes.'

'The children? That's not true. The children are clean. You may be fed up, that's quite likely. But I'm not having you telling lies, just as the natives do. I don't like liars, and that's what you are.'

Diouana said nothing, but her lips quivered. She went up to the bathroom again and undressed. And that is where they found her, dead.

The police came to the conclusion that it was a case of suicide.

The next day, in the sixth column of the fourth page of the papers was a report which was barely noticeable: 'At Antibes, a homesick black woman cut her throat.'

Longing

Diouana,
Our sister,
Born on the banks of our Casamance,
The waters of our King river flow
To other horizons,
And the thundering bar batters against the flanks of our
   Africa.

Diouana,
Our sister,
The slave-ships no longer ride the bar.
Terror, despair, the wild hunt,
The cries, the shouts are silenced,
But echo in our memory.
Diouana,
The bar remains.
Centuries have followed centuries,
And the chains are broken,
Termites have eaten away the yokes.
On the flanks of our Mother
Africa,
Stand slaves' houses
(Monuments to our history).
Diouana, proud African girl,
You carry to your grave
The golden rays of our setting sun,
The dance of ears of fonio,
The waltz of the rice-shoots.

Diouana,
Our sister,
Goddess of the night,
The fragrance of our bushlands,
Our nights of joyful revelry,
Our hard wretched life,
Are better far than serfdom.
Longing for the homeland,
Longing for liberty,
Diouana,
Gleam of our coming dawns,
Like our ancestors, you are victim
Of barter.
In transplantation you die,

Like the coconut-palms and banana-trees
Adorning the shores of Antibes,
Those transplanted and sterile trees.

Diouana,
Our sister,
Light of the days to come,
One day soon
We shall say,
These forests,
These fields,
These rivers,
This land,
Our flesh,
Our bones
Are ours alone.
Image of our Mother Africa,
We lament over your sold body,
You are our
Mother,
Diouana.

12

Tribal Scars or The Voltaique

In the evenings we all go to Mane's place, where we drink mint tea and discuss all sorts of subjects, even though we know very little about them. But recently we neglected the major problems such as the ex-Belgian Congo, the trouble in the Mali Federation, the Algerian War and the next UNO meeting – even women, a subject which normally takes up about a quarter of our time. The reason was that Saer, who is usually so stolid and serious, had raised the question, 'Why do we have tribal scars?'

(I should add that Saer is half Voltaique, half Senegalese; but he has no tribal scars.)

Although not all of us have such scars on our faces, I have never heard such an impassioned discussion, such a torrent of words, in all the time we have been meeting together at Mane's. To hear us, anyone would have thought that the future of the whole continent of Africa was at stake. Every evening for weeks the most fantastic and unexpected explanations were put forward. Some of us went to neighbouring villages and even farther afield to consult the elders and the griots, who are known as the 'encyclopedias' of the region, in an endeavour to plumb the depths of this mystery, which seemed buried in the distant past.

Saer was able to prove that all the explanations were wrong.

Someone said vehemently that 'it was a mark of nobility'; another that 'it was a sign of bondage'. A third declared that 'It was decorative – there was a tribe which would not accept a man or a woman unless they had these distinctive marks on the face and body.' One joker told us with a straight face that: 'Once upon a time, a rich

African chief sent his son to be educated in Europe. The chief's son was a child when he went away, and when he returned he was a man. So he was educated, an intellectual, let us say. He looked down on the tribal traditions and customs. His father was annoyed by this, and wondered how to bring him back into the royal fold. He consulted his chief counsellor. And one morning, out on the square and in front of the people, the son's face was marked with cuts.'

No one believed that story, and the teller was reluctantly obliged to abandon it.

Someone else said: 'I went to the French Institute and hunted around in books, but found nothing. However, I learned that the wives of the gentlemen in high places are having these marks removed from their faces; they go to Europe to consult beauticians. For the new rules for African beauty disdain the old standards of the country; the women are becoming Americanized. It's the spreading influence of the "darkies" of Fifth Avenue, New York. And as the trend develops, tribal scars lose their meaning and importance and are bound to disappear.'

We talked about their diversity, too; about the variety even within one tribe. Cuts were made on the body as well as on the face. This led someone to ask: 'If these tribal scars were signs of nobility, or of high or low caste, why aren't they ever seen in the Americas?'

'Ah, we're getting somewhere at last!' exlaimed Saer, who obviously knew the right answer to his original question, or thought he did.

'Tell us then. We give up,' we all cried.

'All right,' said Saer. He waited while the man on duty brought in glasses of hot tea and passed them round. The room became filled with the aroma of mint.

'So we've got around to the Americas,' Saer began. 'Now, none of the authoritative writers on slavery and the slave trade has ever mentioned tribal scars, so far as I know. In South America, where fetishism and witchcraft as practised by slaves still survive to this day, no tribal scars have ever been seen. Neither do Negroes living in the Caribbean have them, nor in Haita, Cuba, the Dominican

Republic nor anywhere else. So we come back to Black Africa
before the slave trade, to the time of the old Ghana Empire, the
Mali and the Gao Empires, and the cities and kingdoms of
the Hausa, Bournou, Benin, Mossi and so on. Now, not one of the
travellers who visited those places and wrote about them mentions
this practice of tribal scars. So where did it originate?'

By now everyone had stopped sipping hot tea; they were all
listening attentively.

'If we study the history of the slave trade objectively we find that
the dealers sought blacks who were strong and healthy and without
blemish. We find too, among other things, that in the markets here
in Africa and on arrival overseas the slave was inspected, weighed
and evaluated like an animal. No one was inclined to buy merchan-
dise which had any blemish or imperfection, apart from a small
mark which was the stamp of the slave-trader; but nothing else was
tolerated on the body of the beast. For there was also the preparation
of the slave for the auction market; he was washed and polished –
whitened, as they said then – which raised the price. How, then, did
these scars originate?'

We could find no answer. His historical survey had deepened the
mystery for us.

'Go on, Saer, you tell us,' we said, more eager than ever to hear
his story of the origin of tribal scars.

And this is what he told us:

The slave-ship *African* had been anchored in the bay for days,
waiting for a full load before sailing for the Slave States. There were
already more than fifty black men and thirty Negro women down
in the hold. The captain's agents were scouring the country for
supplies. On this particular day only a few of the crew were on
board; with the captain and the doctor, they were all in the latter's
cabin. Their conversation could be heard on deck.

Amoo bent lower and glanced back at the men who were following him. He was a strong, vigorous man with rippling muscles, fit
for any manual work. He gripped his axe firmly in one hand and felt

his long cutlass with the other, then crept stealthily forward. More armed men dropped lithely over the bulwarks, one after the other. Momutu, their leader, wearing a broad-brimmed hat, a blue uniform with red facings, and high black boots, signalled with his musket to surround the galley. The ship's cooper had appeared from nowhere and tried to escape by jumping into the sea. But the blacks who had remained in the canoes seized him and speared him to death.

Fighting had broken out aboard the *African*. One of the crew tried to get to close quarters with the leading attackers and was struck down. The captain and the remaining men shut themselves in the doctor's cabin. Momutu and his band, armed with muskets and cutlasses, besieged the cabin, firing at it now and again. Meanwhile the vessel was being looted. As the shots rang out, the attackers increased in number; canoes left the shore, glided across the water to the *African*, and returned laden with goods.

Momutu called his lieutenants to him – four big fellows armed to the teeth. 'Start freeing the prisoners and get them out of the hold.'

'What about him?' asked his second-in-command, nodding towards Amoo who was standing near the hatchway.

'We'll see about him later,' replied Momutu. 'He's looking for his daughter. Get the hold open – and don't give any arms to the local men. Take the lot!'

The air was heavy with the smell of powder and sweat. Amoo was already battering away at the hatch-covers, and eventually they were broken open with axes and a ram.

Down in the stinking hold the men lay chained together by their ankles. As soon as they had heard the firing they had begun shouting partly with joy, partly from fright. From between-decks, where the women were, came terrified cries. Among all this din, Amoo could make out his daughter's voice. Sweat pouring from him, he hacked at the panels with all his strength.

'Hey, brother, over here!' a man called to him. 'You're in a hurry to find your daughter?'

'Yes,' he answered, his eyes glittering with impatience.

After many hours of hard work the hold was wide open and

Momutu's men had brought up the captives and lined them up on deck, where the ship's cargo for barter had been gathered together: barrels of spirits, boxes of knives, crates containing glassware, silks, parasols and cloth. Amoo had found his daughter, Iome, and the two were standing a little apart from the rest. Amoo knew very well that Momutu had rescued the captives only in order to sell them again. It was he who had lured the *African*'s captain into the bay.

'Now we're going ashore,' Momutu told them. 'I warn you that you are my prisoners. If anyone tries to escape or to kill himself, I'll take the man next in the line and cut him to pieces.'

The sun was sinking towards the horizon and the bay had become a silvery, shimmering sheet of water; the line of trees along the shore stood out darkly. Momutu's men began to put the booty into canoes and take it ashore. Momutu, as undisputed leader, directed operations and gave orders. Some of his men still stood on guard outside the cabin, reminding those inside of their presence by discharging their muskets at the door every few minutes. When the ship had been cleared, Momutu lit a long fuse that ran to two kegs of gunpowder. The captain, finding that all was quiet, started to make his way up top; as he reached the deck, a ball from a musket hit him full in the chest. The last canoes pulled away from the ship, and when they were half-way to the shore the explosions began; then the *African* blew up and sank.

By the time everything had been taken ashore it was quite dark. The prisoners were herded together and a guard set over them, although their hands and feet were still tied. Throughout the night their whisperings and sobs could be heard, punctuated now and then by the sharp crack of a whip. Some distance away, Momutu and his aides were reckoning up their haul, drinking quantities of spirits under the starry sky as they found how well they had done for themselves.

Momutu sent for Amoo to join them.

'You'll have a drink with us, won't you?' said Momutu when Amoo approached with his sleeping daughter on his back (but they only appeared as dim shadows).

'I must be going. I live a long way off and the coast isn't a safe place now. I've been working for you for two months,' said Amoo, refusing a drink.

'Is it true that you killed your wife rather than let her be taken prisoner by slave-traders?' asked one of the men, reeking of alcohol.

'Ahan!'

'And you've risked your life more than once to save your daughter?'

'She's my daughter! I've seen all my family sold into slavery one after another, and taken away into the unknown. I've grown up with fear, fleeing with my tribe so as not to be made a slave. In my tribe there are no slaves, we're all equal.'

'That's because you don't live on the coast,' put in a man, which made Momutu roar with laughter. 'Go on, have a drink! You're a great fighter. I saw how you cut down that sailor. You're good with an axe.'

'Stay with me. You're tough and you know what you want,' said Momutu, passing the keg of spirits to him. Amoo politely declined a drink. 'This is our work,' Momutu went on. 'We scour the grasslands, take prisoners and sell them to the whites. Some captains know me, but I entice others to this bay and some of my men lure the crew off the ship. Then we loot the ship and get the prisoners back again. We kill any whites left on board. It's easy work, and we win all round. I've given you back your daughter. She's a fine piece and worth several iron bars.'

(Until the seventeenth century on the west coast of Africa slaves were paid for with strings of cowries as well as with cheap goods; later, iron bars took the place of cowries. It is known that elsewhere in other markets iron bars have always been the medium of exchange.)

'It's true that I've killed men,' said Amoo, 'but never to take prisoners and sell them as slaves. That's your work, but it isn't mine. I want to get back to my village.'

'He's an odd fellow. He thinks of nothing but his village, his wife and his daughter.'

Amoo could only see the whites of their eyes. He knew that these men would not think twice of seizing himself and his daughter and selling them to the first slave-trader encountered. He was not made in their evil mould.

'I wanted to set off tonight.'

'No,' snapped Momutu. The alcohol was beginning to take effect, but he controlled himself and softened his voice. 'We'll be in another fight soon. Some of my men have gone with the remaining whites to collect prisoners. We must capture them. Then you'll be free to go.'

'I'm going to get her to lie down and have some sleep. She's had a bad time,' said Amoo, moving away with his daughter.

'Has she had something to eat?'

'We've both eaten well. I'll be awake early.'

The two disappeared into the night; but a shadowy figure followed them.

'He's a fine, strong fellow. Worth four kegs.'

'More than that,' added another. 'He'd fetch several iron bars and some other stuff as well.'

'Don't rush it! After the fight tomorrow we'll seize him and his daughter too. She's worth a good bit. We mustn't let them get away. There aren't many of that kind to be found along the coast now.'

A soothing coolness was coming in from the sea. Night pressed close, under a starry sky. Now and then a scream of pain rose sharply, followed by another crack of the whip. Amoo had settled down with Iome some distance away from the others. His eyes were alert, though his face looked sleepy. During the dozen fights he had taken part in to redeem his daughter, Momutu had been able to judge his qualities, his great strength and supple body. Three times three moons ago, slave-hunters had raided Amoo's village and carried off all the able-bodied people. He had escaped their clutches because that day he had been out in the bush. His mother-in-law, who had been spurned because of her elephantiasis, had told him the whole story.

When he had recovered his daughter from the slave-ship, his tears had flowed freely. Firmly holding the girl's wrist and clutching the bloodstained axe in his other hand, his heart had beat fast. Iome, who was nine or ten years old, had wept too.

He had tried to soothe away her fears. 'We're going back to the village. You mustn't cry, but you must do what I tell you. Do you understand?'

'Yes, father.'

'Don't cry any more. It's all over now! I'm here with you.'

And there in the cradle of the night, Iome lay asleep with her head on her father's thigh. Amoo unslung his axe and placed it close at hand. Sitting with his back against a tree, his whole attention was concentrated on the immediate surroundings. At the slightest rustle, his hand went out to grasp his weapon. He dozed a little from time to time.

Even before a wan gleam had lighted the east, Momutu roused his men. Some of them were ordered to take the prisoners and the loot to a safe place. Amoo and Iome kept out of the way. The girl had deep-set eyes and was tall for her age; her hair was parted in the middle and drawn into two plaits which hung down to her shoulders. She clung to her father's side; she had seen her former companions from the slave-ship, and although she may not have known the fate in store for them, the sound of the whips left her in no doubt as to their present state.

'They'll wait for us farther on,' said Momutu, coming across to Amoo. 'We mustn't let ourselves be surprised by the whites' scouting party. Why are you keeping your child with you? You could have left her with one of my men.'

'I'd rather keep her with me. She's very frightened,' answered Amoo, watching the prisoners and escort moving off.

'She's a beautiful girl.'

'Yes.'

'As beautiful as her mother?'

'Not quite.'

Momutu turned away and got the rest of his men, about thirty, on the move. They marched in single column. Momutu was well known among slave-traders, and none of them trusted him. He had previously acted as an agent for some of the traders, then had become a 'master of language' (interpreter), moving between the forts and camps where the captured Negroes were held.

They marched all that morning, with Amoo and his daughter following in the rear. When Iome was tired, her father carried her on his back. He was well aware that a watch was being kept on him The men ahead of him were coarse, sorry-looking creatures; they looked ridiculous, trailing their long muskets. They began to leave the grasslands behind and soon were among tall trees where flocks of vultures perched. No one spoke. All that could be heard was the chattering of birds and now and again a distant, echoing howling. Then they reached the forest, humid and hostile, and Momutu called a halt; he dispersed his men and told them to rest.

'Are you tired, brother?' one of them asked Amoo. 'And what about her?'

Iome raised her thick-lashed eyes towards the man, then looked at her father.

'She's a bit tired,' said Amoo, looking round for a resting-place. He saw a fallen trunk at the foot of a tree and took Iome to it. The man set to keep watch on them remained a little distance away.

Momutu had a few sweet potatoes distributed to the men, and when this meagre meal was over he went to see Amoo.

'How's your daughter?'

'She's asleep,' said Amoo, who was carving a doll out of a piece of wood.

'She's a strong girl,' said Momutu, sitting down beside him and taking off his broad-brimmed hat. His big black boots were all muddy. 'We'll have a rest and wait for them here. They're bound to come this way.'

Amoo was more and more on his guard. He nodded, but kept his eyes on Iome in between working at the piece of wood, which was gradually taking shape.

'After that you'll be free to go. Do you really want to go back to your village?'

'Yes.'

'But you haven't anybody left there,' said Momutu, and without waiting for Amoo to reply went on, 'I once had a village, too, on the edge of a forest. My mother and father lived there, many relatives – a whole clan! We had meat to eat and sometimes fish. But over the years, the village declined. There was no end to lamentations. Ever since I was born I'd heard nothing but screams, seen mad flights into the bush or the forest. You go into the forest, and you die from some disease; you stay in the open, and you're captured to be sold into slavery. What was I to do? Well, I made my choice. I'd rather be with the hunters than the hunted.'

Amoo, too, knew that such was life. You were never safe, never sure of seeing the next day dawn. But what he did not understand was the use made of the men and women who were taken away. It was said that the whites used their skins for making boots.

They talked for a long time, or rather Momutu talked without stopping. He boasted of his exploits and his drinking bouts. As Amoo listened, he became more and more puzzled about Momutu's character. He was like some petty warlord, wielding power by force and constraint. Eventually, after what seemed a very long time to Amoo, a man came to warn the chief that the whites were approaching. Momutu gave his orders – kill them all, and hold their prisoners. In an instant the forest fell silent; only the neutral voice of the wind could be heard.

The long file of black prisoners came into view, led by four Europeans each armed with two pistols and a culverin. The prisoners, men and women, were joined together by a wooden yoke bolted round the neck and attached to the man in front and the one behind. Three more Europeans brought up the rear, and a fourth, probably ill, was being carried in a litter by four natives.

A sudden burst of firing from up in the trees echoed long and far. This was followed by screams and confused fighting. Amoo took advantage to fell the man guarding him and, taking his daughter by the hand, slipped away into the forest.

They crossed streams and rivers, penetrating ever deeper into the forest but heading always to the south-east. Amoo's knife and axe had never been so useful as during this time. They travelled chiefly at night, never in broad daylight, avoiding all human contact.

Three weeks later they arrived at the village – about thirty huts huddled together between the bush and the source of a river. There were few inhabitants about at that hour of the day; besides, having been frequently drained of its virile members, the village was sparsely populated. When Amoo and Iome reached the threshold of his mother-in-law's hut, the old woman limped out and her cries drew other people, many of them feeble. They were terrified at first, but stood uttering exclamations of joy and surprise when they saw Amoo and Iome. Tears and questions mingled as they crowded round. Iome's grandmother gathered her up and took her into the hut like a most precious possession, and the girl replied to her questions between floods of tears.

The elders sent for Amoo to have a talk and tell them of his adventures.

'All my life, and since before my father's life,' said one of the oldest present, 'the whole country has lived in the fear of being captured and sold to the whites. The whites are barbarians.'

'Will it ever end?' queried another. 'I have seen all my children carried off, and I can't remember how many times we have moved the village. We can't go any farther into the forest . . . there are the wild beasts, diseases . . .'

'I'd rather face wild beasts than slave-hunters,' said a third man. 'Five or six rains ago, we felt safe here. But we aren't any longer. There's a slave camp only three-and-a-half days' march from the village.'

They fell silent; their wrinkled, worn and worried faces bore the mark of their epoch. They discussed the necessity to move once again. Some were in favour, others pointed out the danger of living in the heart of the forest without water, the lack of strong men, and the family graves that would have to be abandoned. The patriarch, who had the flat head and thick neck of a degenerate, proposed that they should spend the winter where they were but send a group to seek another suitable site. It would be sheer madness to leave without having first discovered and prepared a place to go to. There were also the customary sacrifices to be made. Finally, all the men agreed on this course of action. During the short time they would remain there, they would increase cultivation and hold all the cattle in common, keeping the herd in an enclosure. The patriarch was of the opinion that the old women could be used to keep a watch on the village.

The return of Amoo and Iome had put new life into them. They started working communally, clearing and weeding the ground and mending the fences. The men set off for work together and returned together. The women busied themselves too; some did the cooking while others kept a look-out for any surprise visit by 'procurers'. (Procurers were native agents, recognizable by their uniform in the colours of the nation they worked for; they were commonly called 'slave-hunters'.) No one looked in the direction of the sea without a feeling of apprehension.

The rains came, and the fertile, bountiful earth gave life to the seeds that had been sown. Although the villagers went about their work with no visible sign of worry or fear, they were always on the alert for an attack, knowing it was bound to come sooner or later.

Amoo shared his hut with Iome and always slept with a weapon close at hand. Even a harmless gust of wind sent the girl into a panic. Amoo put his whole heart into his work; Iome, by general agreement, was allowed to rest as much as possible, and she gradually recovered from her ordeal. Her black cheeks shone again, tiny folds formed round her neck and her flat little breasts began to fill out.

Days and weeks slipped by peacefully. The narrow, cultivated strips of land, wrenched from the grip of nature after long struggles, were giving promise of a good harvest. The cassava plants were in bud; the people were beginning to get in stocks of palm-oil, butter, beans and honey, in fact everything they would need in the new village. The prospecting party returned, having discovered an excellent site at the foot of the mountains but above the grasslands, and not far from a running stream. The soil was good, there was plenty of pasture, and the children would be safe from the 'procurers'.

Everyone was very pleased with the prospect. The patriarch named the day for departure, and the feeling of safety in the near future led to a relaxation of precautions. Fires, previously forbidden during the hours of darkness for fear of betraying the village, now glowed at night; laughter rang out, and children dared to wander out of sight of their parents, for the adults were thinking only of the departure. They could count the days now. In the council hut there were discussions on which was the favourable sign for the move. Each and everyone was attending to the household gods, the totems and the family graves.

Yet it was not a sacred day, but one like any other. The sun was shining brightly, the tender green leaves of the trees were rustling in the wind, the clouds frolicked in the sky, the humming-birds were gaily seeking food, and the monkeys especially were gambolling in the trees. The whole village was enjoying this glorious day, the kind that can tempt a traveller to stay awhile, a long while.

And it happened on that particular day! On that day the 'procurers' suddenly appeared. The frightened animals instinctively fled madly into the forest; men, women and children gave terrified screams on hearing the firing and scattered in panic, having but one thought, to flee to the only retreat open to them – the forest.

Amoo, grasping his axe, pushed Iome and her grandmother before him. But the old, handicapped woman could make only slow progress. They had fled between the huts and the enclosure and gained the edge of the village, and then Amoo had come face to face with one of Momutu's lieutenants. Amoo was the quicker, and struck him down. But now a whole pack was in pursuit.

Amoo went deeper into the forest, where the thick undergrowth

and overhanging branches made progress even slower. Still, if Amoo
had been alone, he could have escaped. But he could not abandon
his child. He thought of his wife. He had killed her so that she
should not be taken. His mother-in-law reminded him of his wife.
To abandon the old woman would be abandoning his wife. Time
and again, the old woman stopped to get her breath; her thick
leg was becoming ever weightier to drag along. Amoo helped
her as best he could, while Iome stuck to his side, not saying a
word.

An idea came to Amoo. He stopped, took Iome gently by the
chin and gazed at her for a long time, for what seemed an eternity.
His eyes filled with tears.

'Mother,' he said, 'we can't go any farther. Ahead, there's death
for all three of us. Behind, there's slavery for Iome and me.'

'I can't go a step farther,' said the old woman, taking her grand-
daughter by the hand. She raised a distraught face to Amoo.

'Mother, Iome can escape them. You both can. Your skin is no
longer any use, the whites can't make boots with it.'

'But if Iome's left alone, she'll die. And what about you?'

'You go free. What happens to me is my affair.'

'You're not going to kill us?' exclaimed the woman.

'No, mother. But I know what to do so that Iome stays free. I
must do it quickly. They're getting near, I can hear their voices.'

A thunderbolt seemed to burst in his head and the ground to slip
away from him. He took a grip on himself, seized his knife and
went to a particular bush (the Wolof call it *Bantamare*; its leaves
have antiseptic properties), wrenched off a handful of the large
leaves and returned to the other two, who had been watching him
wonderingly.

His eyes blurred with tears as he looked at his daughter. 'You
mustn't be afraid, Iome.'

'You're not going to kill her as you did her mother?' exclaimed
his mother-in-law again.

'No. Iome, this is going to hurt, but you'll never be a slave. Do
you understand?'

The child's only answer was to stare at the blade of the knife. She remembered the slave-ship and the bloodstained axe.

Swiftly, Amoo gripped the girl between his strong legs and began making cuts all over her body. The child's cries rang through the forest; she screamed till she had no voice left. Amoo just had time to finish before the slave-hunters seized him. He had wrapped the leaves all round the girl. With the other captured villagers, Amoo was taken down to the coast. Iome returned to the village with her grandmother, and thanks to the old woman's knowledge of herbs Iome's body soon healed; but she still bore the scars.

Months later, the slave-hunters returned to the village; they captured Iome but let her go again. She was worth nothing, because of the blemishes on her body.

The news spread for leagues around. People came from the remotest villages to consult the grandmother. And over the years and the centuries a diversity of scars appeared on the bodies of our ancestors.

And that is how our ancestors came to have tribal scars. They refused to be slaves.

Glossary

babouche	a slipper
bilal	muezzin, he who calls the people to prayer and looks after a mosque
boubou	a voluminous garment worn by Muslims
burnous	a long cloak with a hood to it
derhems	a unit of currency in Senegal
El Hadj	title of a Muslim who has made the pilgrimage to the Holy City of Mecca
griot	member of a low caste of praise-singers
imam	religious in charge of a mosque
inch' Allah!	God willing!
Kaâba	sacred building at Mecca, and the Muslim Holy of Holies
kora	a kind of harp
kuskus	*couscous* in French, a dish of granulated flour steamed over broth, with pieces of mutton added
marabout	a holy man; also his tomb
m'ba	a screened-off area
salamalec	a greeting of Turkish origin
tacousane	Muslim afternoon prayer
taleb	teacher in a Koranic school
timis	Muslim sunset prayer
veudieu	co-wife